MAD DAWN WINTER

AMRA PAJALIĆ

MELBOURNE, AUSTRALIA

https://www.pishukinpress.com/

First Published 2026 by Pishukin Press

Cover design: Created using Canva elements, cover image attribution photo by naban55 from pixabay via Canva

Editing Support: I use ProWritingAid and Sudowrite, both of which incorporate artificial intelligence, to support the editing and revision process. I'm committed to transparency and quality, and AI is used as a creative aid while I retain full control over all artistic and editorial decisions.

For content and trigger warnings please go towww.amrapajalic.com/themes

Quality control: We care about producing error-free books. If you discover a typo or formatting issue, please contact admin@pishukinpress.com

Paperback Edition: 9781922871619

Content Warnings

www.amrapajalic.com/themes.html

1-Exiled

I stirred, coming to consciousness slowly, aware of the warm body cradling mine. Ninu was behind me, his arm beneath my head as I lay on my side. I smiled, lifting myself to peer at him. He was sleeping, his dark eyelashes resting on his cheekbones.

'Time to wake up sleepyhead.' I kissed him gently on the cheek.

He stirred, his dark eyelashes fluttering open, his hazel eyes watching me. 'Already?'

I nodded, glancing at the clock beside me. It was six a.m. I got up and went to the bathroom first, leaving Ninu to come to consciousness. I was in the shower when he stepped in behind me, his hands cupping my breasts.

'Let me help you.' He took the soap and lathered my torso while I giggled.

'And this is why I set the alarm so early.' I turned toward him, wrapping my arms around his neck as I kissed him.

After we dressed, Ninu packing the change of clothes he'd brought for the weekend. 'You staying for breakfast?' I shrugged on my cardigan, the chill of morning penetrating.

He shook his head as he put on his shoes. 'I'll get takeaway on the way home.'

It was a hour's drive from the town of Riverwood back to St Albans. After my mother and Emir found out about my dating Ninu, they gave me an ultimatum: leave my family home or break up with Ninu. I chose Ninu. Thankfully, my mentor Alyssa Jones had helped me find a journalism cadetship in the small country town of Riverwood and within a week I was suddenly a fully emancipated adult—even though I was twenty-three years old.

I followed Ninu to the porch. As I opened the door, the sun was peeking over the trees in front of the house, the frigid blast of air piercing my skin. I walked him to his ute. 'See you Friday.' I leaned in to kiss Ninu through the open window.

He kissed me back, his hand cupping the back of my head. I watched as he drove off, standing on the porch, taking in the vista before me. It was so peaceful living in the country. It was still a novelty after two weeks in.

I returned to the kitchen with the faded black and white checked linoleum floor that now looked grey, and aqua green cabinets that were scratched and faded. There was a vinyl table and chrome white padded chairs. The kitchen must've once been a modern masterpiece in the 1950s when the house was built, but was now neglected and old, like so much of the house. To me, it was still a novelty. It was my first time living on my own and I loved every piece of the three-bedroom house I was renting.

I ate my toast and tea, then briskly completed my house-work. Now that I was living on my own, I'd learnt it was best to wash dishes and make my bed before leaving the house in the morning, so I could relax in the evening after work.

By the time I finished, an hour had passed and when I stepped back out onto the porch, the sun was fully out; the chill easing. I walked down the stairs and into the car that Ninu had helped me buy when I moved to Riverwood. As I backed out of the driveway my eyes caught on the white weatherboard house, the white paint peeling. I wouldn't have been able to afford to live in a house by myself in the suburbs, but in this small country town, my salary stretched far enough to accommodate the rent and a comfortable lifestyle.

I eased into my Toyota and turned onto River Road, the main road that ran parallel to the Guru River that hugged the town of Riverwood, the sun winking off the murky surface of the water as I drove. I passed by the *Welcome to Riverwood* sign, population 2,985, when I saw a woman walking with red roses in her arms. She turned down the path by the river. I stopped the car on the shoulder of the road, took the camera from the passenger seat beside me, and followed.

I'd walked down by the river yesterday with Ninu. I'd been told there was a beautiful gorge for swimming and we'd found it walking from my house, reaching the clifftop overlooking it. We'd had to climb down a winding path among the brush, but now as I followed the woman, I realised this was the other path to get to the gorge that most people from town used.

When Ninu and I had reached the gorge, we'd found a tree with flowers tied to it, a tribute to someone who had passed, probably drowned. I'd thought then it might make a good story about tributes and the people who left them, but to do that I'd need to track down the person leaving the tribute and now she'd landed in my lap, so to speak.

The woman walked to the tree and took down the dry and old flowers, tying the new bouquet with a red ribbon. I lifted the camera to my eye, framing a shot of her standing there, holding her hands up as if she were praying, the clifftop in the background behind her. The woman rubbed her hand over her face in a familiar gesture. I lifted my eye from the camera viewfinder and looked at her. Almost like how Muslims pray.

I let the camera hang around my neck and approached her.

'Excuse me,' I called, not wanting to startle her.

The woman glanced at me, but didn't respond.

'I work at the Riverwood Times and wanted to talk to you about your tribute.'

The woman walked toward me. I waited, a smile on my face. She brushed past me, continued walking without staying a word. I turned to look, bewildered by her cold shoulder. When she'd vanished from sight back up the road, I turned around and walked to the tribute. I framed the shot of the red roses tied with the red ribbon to the pole, the yellow grassland on the banks swishing in the wind, the river murky and undulating in the current. I made a note to ask for drowning statistics at the police station. The breeze fluttered over me, raising goose pimples on my arms. I rubbed my arms, feeling as if someone had walked over my grave.

I dawdled at the gorge, giving the woman time to leave so I wouldn't bump into her, feeling slightly embarrassed like I'd committed a faux pas. Who was she? While the townspeople I'd met so far viewed me as an exotic species with my ethnic name, Seka Torlak, the cause of much curiosity in this mostly

Anglo town, everyone had been friendly and hospitable. This was the first time someone had been rude, and I didn't know what I had done to cause this kind of reaction. Was she one of those who hated refugees and saw me as an interloper because of my migrant background? While no residents had been outwardly rude, I had overheard some conversations in the street and the way some townsfolk viewed migrants.

Fifteen minutes later I parked in front of the newspaper office, a one-storey building on the main road, the shop front windows lettered with a cursive sign: The Riverwood Times, Printing Office. Behind the sheer white curtains were the offices where the journalists and editors worked, as well as the printing press that used the centuries-old method of hot lead printing. Each Thursday, the yellow-bricked building shook to the rhythm of a massive 1894 steel printing press while volunteers folded the pages, their hands black with ink by day's end. The town of Riverwood and its surrounding regions have been served by the newspaper since 1883, when the town was populated and the building was constructed in 1893, as evidenced by the concrete round sign on top of the building.

I walked in and sat at my desk. In my in-tray was a handwritten column by the reverend who this week was using the lost lambs from the Carlisle farm as a metaphor about God seeking to encourage recalcitrant parishioners to find their way home to the church. I squinted as I read it, fighting to decipher his cramped handwriting. This had been my first steep learning curve, that it was more than just the reporters that contributed to the newspaper. Contributions came from many of the pillars of the community, including the mayor, the police sergeant, the progress association, members of parliament, teachers and schoolkids, and sporting club secretaries. There was even a gossip column on the back page reporting on locals' bloopers, from the principal wearing a skirt that flew up in the wind to reveal her red lacy underwear, to the farmer who rode his bicycle home from the pub and ended up headfirst in a nettle bush.

I was deep in thought, and the tapping didn't intrude on my consciousness until he was beside me.

'Hello dear,' Mayor Shane Otis said, looking down at me with what should be a benign smile above his ginger and salted beard.

'Hello Mayor Otis.' I wanted to stand, but he'd blocked me in with his cane resting between my legs. 'I've got my column.' He reached into the front pocket of his white suit and delicately took out a folded sheet of paper.

As he handed it to me, I avoided touching his fingertips. I placed it in my in-tray.

'Tut, tut.' He lifted his cane and tapped the in-tray. 'I'd like you to proofread it now, please. Don't want you to have to interpret any minor details and get them wrong.'

I sighed, unfolding the sheet and reading the neatly hand-written sheet.

'The council has made the careful and circumspect decision not to fund the local library at this time, in order to ensure that the public works, such as the road repairs on the main road in order not to hinder and impede the population's transit and movement between town and surrounding farms.'

'I think we could do some pruning here,' I said, reaching for my pen. 'For example, careful and circumspect mean the same thing. Which one would you like to use?'

The Mayor's nostrils flared as his cheeks flushed. 'Both, thank you. Perhaps as a native speaker you don't have the sophistication to understand the nuances between the two—'

'There are no nuances—'

Art fluttered out of his office. 'How are you, Mayor Otis?' he asked, standing behind my chair.

'Not very well at all, Art. This young chit is critiquing my article, which is not the service that I request. The council pays advertising dollars for our message to be heard across the shire.'

'Of course, of course,' Art said, taking the column and glancing at it. 'Beautifully written as always, Mayor. We'll publish that exactly as it is.'

'Yes, do.' Mayor Otis glared at me once more before stalking out, his cane tapping furiously on the ground as he slowly shuffled out.

'He—' I began.

Art raised his hand to his lips, shushing me, as he watched the Mayor leave the office. When the door closed, he turned back to me. 'The Mayor is very pedantic about his column and the council advertising is 50 percent of our operating costs. So we will publish it exactly as it is written.'

I sighed with frustration and nodded.

'Exactly as it is. Which means not even a comma is to be changed.' Art tapped at the red mark where I had included a proofreading note for a comma to break up the sentence. 'We pick our battles, my dear.' He patted my arm.

I nodded again. Art was the boss and owner. Even though typing that column was going to test my patience, this wasn't worth fighting. I returned to my inbox and lost track of time.

'Seka, someone here for you,' Karen, the receptionist, called out a while later.

I stood and walked to the counter where a thin woman with white permed hair was waiting. 'My seven year old granddaughter won a national short story competition,' she declared proudly.

'How wonderful! Let me get my notebook.' This had been the other surprise. The day-to-day achievements of the locals were regular features in the newspaper. Soon after arriving when I'd complained about Karen hand-balling me puff-pieces, my editor, Art Monday, corrected my misconceptions. 'Locals read this newspaper and they want to know about the lives and achievements of their own.'

After I'd jotted notes about the woman's granddaughter, I returned to my desk and typed up the reverend's column.

Karen called me again. I stood and approached the counter where two women stood. By their resemblance, they were mother and daughter. They had the same shade of brown hair. The younger woman had hers cut to the nape with the ends curling out, while the older had hers smoothed into a bun. They watched me approach with identical dark brown eyes. 'How can I help you?'

I walked over and offered my hand to the women. 'Seka Torlak.'

'I'm Millie Roberts. And this is my mother, Michelle Hayes. Do you have time to talk?' We shook hands.

I glanced over at the proofs, waiting for my approval. I turned back to Millie, about to tell her no, but there was a look of desperation and hope in her eyes that stilled the words on my tongue. 'Of course, come in.' I held open the swinging door and gestured them in. I walked over to my desk and offered Mrs Hayes a seat and took a chair from another table and offered it to Millie. 'Would you like coffee?'

The women shook their heads.

'What can I do to help you?'

'We're here about my brother.' Millie slipped out a photo of a young man and handed it to me. 'Ben was murdered and no one was ever arrested over his death.'

'I'm very sorry.' I looked at the small black-and-white photo of a young man in a pinstriped grey suit, his hair swept to the side, a wide smile on his face. Curious about the writing on the back, I flipped it over and found the inscription 'Ben, 1972.' I looked at Millie, confused.

'He passed away three months after that photo was taken. Having served in Vietnam, he returned and landed a job as a surveyor at the council while he finished his engineering degree. He bought the suit he's wearing from his first paycheck. He was so proud.' Mrs Hayes smiled sadly.

'How do you want me to help?' I asked.

'It's been twenty six years since his death and we want you to write about him. He was found beaten to the death at the footy stadium change room. They did an inquest and concluded that a seasonal worker passing through must have killed him, but I've never believed it.' Millie stopped talking, looking at her mother with concern.

Pain lined Mrs. Hayes' face, but her eyes remained clear. 'Someone in this town knows what happened to Ben, but they said nothing. I want them to tell the truth. My husband died five years ago and I have cancer. The doctors said I have six months. I want to know who killed Ben and why before I leave this earth. Will you help?' Mrs Hayes put her hand on my arm.

The pain emanated from her hand and into my body like a blood transfusion. I recognised this pain, had carried it with me since Srebrenica. I had decided to be a journalist so that I could write about things that mattered and make a change in the world. This was my chance.

'Yes, I'll write about him.'

Millie and Mrs Hayes smiled widely.

'I knew you were the one who would do it.' Mrs Hayes patted my arm. 'I read the article you wrote in The Age about your father and fiancé.'

I survived the genocide in Srebrenica, where the killing of 8,372 men and boys took place, including my fiancé and father. Those killed were buried in mass graves, many of their bodies still undiscovered. It was the event that both defined and haunted me.

I walked Millie and Mrs Hayes out after I had written their phone numbers and address. 'I'll call to make a time for an interview after I speak to the police sergeant and view the inquest report.'

I returned to my desk and quickly finished typing the column before searching through the microfiche file that contained all the previous issues. There was a short write up about Ben Hayes' death in 1972 stating he was found in the footy club change rooms and that the police were investigating leads. Two months later, an even smaller article that the police were concluding a drifter was responsible.

I was confused. Usually local stories captured large interest. Why was this one barely covered? A murder in a local town should have been earth-shattering, let alone the death of a former soldier. I knew about Australia's involvement in the Vietnam War from Ninu, who'd had an uncle that served. Soldiers were conscripted based on their birthday to provide a compulsory twelve month service as National Servicemen, or Nasho's as they were colloquially called, many of them returning to Australia with extreme PTSD that was never treated or addressed.

While some soldiers who arrived home on the HMAS Sydney were given a parade, those, like Ninu's uncle, who had arrived home on a plane when negative sentiment about the war had arisen, were covertly flown in under the cover of night. They were then transported on a bus with darkened windows to protect them from protestors. Ninu told me that his uncle had attempted to enter a RSL Club and join other war veterans. Those inside turned their backs and told him he didn't fight a real war. The Vietnam War was the first war fought without clear battle lines, instead the two sides fought in jungles and villages, with soldiers and civilians both being casualties.

There was a photo of Ben in the newspaper from before he left for the war. Now, as I compared the photo his mother had handed me of him before he died and the photo printed before he was a soldier, I hardly recognised him. As if the year of soldiering in the jungle had transformed his physiology, leaving the planes of his face stark and chiseled, his brown eyes squinty as if he viewed everything before him with suspicion, deep lines across his forehead, and his lips thinner as if they were constantly pressing down on each other from tension.

Was the story under-reported because he was a Nasho, or was there something else at play? I was drafting my notes when Karen dropped another sheet in my in-tray. Needing a break, I lifted it and saw it was the weekly crime write up from the police sergeant. I looked up and saw the blue-shirted back disappear through the front door. I took my notebook and speed-walked to the door. He was in front of the shop next door, River's Edge cafe.

'Liam,' I called.

He turned, his green eyes sparkling as he looked at me. 'Seka, you can't already be having trouble with my column. I typed it for you.'

I snorted with laughter. On my first day, he overheard me whining about deciphering the reverend's incoherent hand-writing.

'No, it's not that. I wanted to ask you about the gorge.'

'I was just about to have a coffee. Want to join me?' He nodded his head toward the cafe, his auburn hair gleaming in the sun.

'Sure.' He held the door open for me. We ordered at the counter and sat at a back table, neither of us keen on being visible in the front window.

'I had a visit from Mille Hayes this morning. She wants me to write about her son, Ben. He was murdered—'

Liam put his hand up to stop me. 'I know about Millie. She's been calling the police regularly about her son's murder.'

'And?'

'And I reviewed his file. He told his mother he was going to the pub, but never turned up. He was found at the footy changing rooms, but we could never determine why he was there. No one came forward to confirm they were meeting with him. The investigation was also hampered by the fact that it was the Royal Melbourne Weekend and the footy games were cancelled. No one found him for three days. His mother assumed he'd gone to the show with mates and forgotten to tell her. It was only when his body was found on the Tuesday by the footy association secretary that Millie found out he'd been in town the whole time. The investigation was completed. There was nothing to go on.'

'I'd still like to write about it. See if I can shake loose some new leads.'

Liam sighed. 'You know that Millie has cancer.'

'She told me.'

'You could give a dying woman false hope.'

'There is no such thing as false hope,' I snapped. 'When someone dies and you don't know how or why, you can never move on. You are in constant limbo, always searching for loss. Giving her one shot at actually finding out something is the greatest kindness.'

'I'm sorry. I read the article you wrote about your father and fiancé in the national paper.'

I shredded a napkin with my hands, looking over his shoulder.

'I guess I know a little about that, too.'

I met his gaze.

'My mother ran off when I was a kid. It's been thirty years, but every day I expect her to walk through the doors.'

'Have you tried finding her?' I asked.

He smiled ruefully. 'Constantly, but she probably remarried and changed her name. I tell myself I have to just wait and if she's interested in seeing me, she knows where I am.' He took a deep breath. 'Okay. I'll do it. I'll reopen the case. Come by the office this afternoon and pick up a copy of the inquest report.'

I nodded, feeling slightly teary. 'I'll arrange an interview with Millie. Get photos of her, maybe at the footy stadium.'

'She has a tribute that she updates every week. You can't miss it, it's on a stand with pot plants.'

The mention of the tribute made me flashback to this morning. 'I wanted to ask you about the gorge. Have there been many drownings?'

'I'll have to look up the official statistics. I think there was a tourist a few years before my time in the office.'

'No, this would be a local. There is a tribute that is updated every day by a woman with silver black hair. She leaves red roses tied with a red ribbon.'

'That's Mad Dawn Winter.'

I recoiled.

'Sorry, that's what everyone calls her. Dawn Winter lives on the Winter Farm, the one next to your house. She's been here since I was a kid. She's been in and out of psychiatric hospitals her whole life, so people call her mad.'

'Who is she leaving the tribute for?'

Liam shrugged. 'Who knows? She's been doing it ever since I was a kid. My Dad told me that we should respect her and leave her to her grief, whether it's real or imaginary. Growing up, some kids destroyed the tribute completely. Dawn was inconsolable. She didn't stop crying and ended up back in hospital. Her husband, Jack, was furious. The gorge is technically on their property. While she was in hospital, he set up camp at the gorge with a shotgun, living there like a wild man, unshaven and unkept as he cooked on a campfire. Anytime the locals attempted to come and swim, he chased them off. My father and other parents spoke to him, begged for peace. He didn't relent until his wife came from the hospital. He vowed that if anyone ever tore down the tribute again, he'd put up a fence and close it off permanently. No one dared to test his pledge.'

I felt better, realising that Dawn didn't dislike me. She'd just spent so long being a source of ridicule to the townspeople that she'd learnt to keep everyone at a distance.

'Can she hear?' I wondered if I could interview her.

'She's not deaf.'

'So she can speak, but chooses not to?' I attempted clarifying.

'I assume she can,' Liam said. 'But I've never heard her. I've seen her with her daughter and she responds to her daughter's questions. She just says nothing.'

'Do you know why she doesn't speak? Was she injured?'

'Maybe there's more to it,' Liam shrugged, 'but I just always assumed she can't. I'll check the archives and see if I can pull anything up about deaths in the gorge.'

'Thanks.' As I walked back to the office, I couldn't stop mulling over the mystery of Mad Dawn Winter. Why was she mad and why didn't she speak? And were the two connected?

2-Lost

I drove down the River Road, feeling a spark of joy as the river shimmered on the river. Riverwood reminded me of Srebrenica with the mountains a dramatic background behind the town, the forest framing the edges of the town, and the river cutting through the centre. I got to the driveway leading to my house. There were two mailboxes next to each other: a white mailbox with peeling paint that was for the house I rented, and a koala mailbox for my neighbours. A red car stopped and a dark-haired woman left her car idling as she got out and opened the koala mailbox. I hadn't stopped to check my mail for a few days and this was a good chance to talk to the neighbours.

I parked my white car next to hers and got out. 'I'm Seka Torlak. I'm renting the house.' I pointed to the white house whose roof was visible behind the trees.

'The journalist.' The dark-haired woman smiled, looking much younger and less severe. 'Azra Winters.' She offered her hand.

'Azra is a Bosnian name,' I said, surprised to hear it in this small country town.

'My mother is Bosnian. Everyone calls her Dawn, but her real name is Dženana.'

Goose pimples raised on my skin. Dawn was praying in the Muslim way at the tribute.

'I met her at the gorge the other day. I tried talking to her, but...'

'She doesn't talk.' Azra looked over my shoulder to where her house was. 'She had a hard time and hasn't spoken for many years.'

'Maybe she'd like to talk to someone in her mother tongue.'

'I can ask.' Azra took her mail from the car.

'Great.' I opened my mailbox as Azra drove off. It was empty, as I expected, but at least my ruse had given me more information.

As I got back in my car and drove up the driveway to my house, I wondered about Dževahira. Liam told me she hadn't spoken for decades. I couldn't help but wonder why. What had stopped her from speaking?

I walked into the kitchen and opened the fridge. This was the part of living alone that I was still getting used to. When I'd lived at home, it was my mother who did the lion's share of the cooking. While I'd helped with managing the household, cooking had not been my forte. I took out the pastizzi that Ninu had brought from his mother and that were leftover. Whenever he came up for the weekend, she sent him with food that would last a few days. It meant that early in the week I didn't have to cook, but by Thursday and Friday I was hitting the takeaway options on the way home.

I placed them in the oven to heat and sat at the kitchen table. Before coming home, I had collected the inquest file from the police station. I opened it up and read.

Ben had been found laying in the middle of the floor. His arms were splayed out and his eyes unseeing. His face was mangled and bruised.

The coroner concluded he'd been murdered sometime in the early hours of the morning. That he'd been beaten to death. There was a footprint visible on Ben's stomach that's matched a size 12 shoe so the perpetrator was probably about 180 centimetres or more.

I pictured Ben rolling around on the ground, being pushed around by the force of the kicking and stomping on his body. Slowly, he would move less and less as the kicks mounted up, until soon he was just lying prostrate on the ground.

His ribs were broken, he had a fracture of his right arm, probably from a defensive wound. His nose was broken, his eye sockets crushed. While he suffered internal injuries from all those, the fatal blow was a kick to the head that caused a brain haemorrhage.

I finished reading the report and stared vacantly into space. Why did the police conclude it was a drifter when the injuries suggested that this was more than one perpetrator? It was something to ask Liam in the morning.

The oven timer dinged, and I took out the pastizzi. They were piping hot, so I transferred them to a plate and took a glass of lemonade outside on the porch, eating and watching the scenery behind me.

I hadn't been long enough in Riverwood to think about my future, but I could get used to this view. Maybe Ninu and I should think about making our future here. After all, he could buy a farm somewhere nearby, and I could continue working at the newspaper. I smiled softly as I thought about my future.

It was an early night tonight for me.

In the morning, I ate my breakfast quickly and poured my coffee into an esky. I drove to the gorge and parked further away from the path amongst the trees, wanting my car to be hidden.

I walked down the path and sat on a rock near the tribute. As expected, Dawn came by just as the sun was warming. She saw me and hesitated in her step, before walking on as if I wasn't there. I waited until she'd laid her flowers and completed her prayers before approaching.

'Dževahira, my name is Seka Toralk. I spoke to your daughter Azra last night, and she told me your name,' I said in Bosnian.

Dawn looked at me with surprise, before a smile of delight lit up her face. She offered her hand and enthusiastically shook mine.

'I know you don't talk, but I got this so you can share your answers.' I held up a notebook and pen.

Dawn nodded gladly. We sat on the rocks emerging on the shore.

'How long have you lived in Riverwood?' I asked.

Dawn wrote in the notebook and held it up. *1970.*

'That's a long time. How did you come to live here?'

Parents were sharecrop farmers. Fell pregnant. Married Jack.

'My boyfriend is Maltese. When my mother and brother found out I was dating him, they told me to leave him or leave home. That's why I'm in Riverwood.'

Dawn's face clouded, the lines around her mouth deeper with grief.

Me too. Parents disinherit. Leave Riverwood. Leave me.

'I'm so sorry.' I took her hand in mine and clutched it.

She looked out at the gorge. I wondered what her life must be like. To be so lonely. Not to talk to anyone. To have lost family. Was this what my future was heading to?

'What was life like in those early days?'

Very hard. Wake up early. Work very hard. Australian sun very harsh. People very cruel.

I could only wonder at the cruelty she was subjected to.

'I want to know more about your story. To write about it in the newspaper. Us Bosnians have to stick together.'

Not to write in newspaper. Just for you.

'Okay.' I nodded. 'This is just between us. You must have so many stories.'

I'll bring something for you tomorrow. Meet me here.

'Okay.'

Dawn got up. She hesitated, before turning around and hugging me. As she let go, I saw a tear seep from her eye. She walked up the path from the gorge. I stood and followed her. I wondered what she would give me tomorrow.

I looked at my watch. My first appointment of the day allowed me enough time. I drove through town and to the east, where the footy stadium was located.

Mrs Hayes and her daughter Millie were already at the streetlight banister in front of the club, next to a triangle shelf that was lined with brightly coloured pot plants. Mrs Hayes weeded the plants with quick hands and then lifted a watering can, carefully pouring water into each pot.

I got out of the car and took the camera with me. As I approached, I heard Mrs Hayes speaking. I lifted my camera and framed the shot of Mrs Hayes speaking to Ben, telling him about her garden, and that she had visited their former neighbour in a nursing home. Millie stood to the side and watched as her mother gingerly caressed the leaves of the flowers, which were the surrogate that she lavished with a mother's love. When she finished watering, they both bowed their heads and prayed, their movements synchronised from thirty years of practice.

I looked over at the changing room block. The main building was a large one-storey building where the footy club events were held. There was a bar operating on the weekends during the on-season when games were played. The changing rooms were a separate block built of red brick, a remnant from when the footy club was originally built in the 1900s.

I would wait until Michelle, and her mother had left before exploring inside. They finished praying, and we walked over to the bench near the double doors that led to the footy club. Mrs Hayes sat slowly, Michelle helping her, lines on her face etched with pain.

I interviewed Mrs Hayes, getting a feel for Ben as a person before the war, his transformation as a soldier, and his hopes and dreams for the future upon his return to Australia. Quotes circling my head as I thought about the draft article.

'I read the inquest report. You don't have any idea what he might have been doing at the footy club on the Friday night?'

Mrs Hayes shook her head. 'Maybe he was meeting someone for a game, or to run around with the ball, but none of his mates confirmed they were meeting with him.'

Millie looked down at her lap as we spoke.

'And when he didn't come home on Saturday, you assumed he was at the Melbourne Show?'

Mrs Hayes nodded. 'I thought maybe he'd met someone out and made the spontaneous decision to leave. We didn't have all this technology then. If someone tried to call home and you didn't answer, we didn't have an answering machine to take a message. I thought maybe he'd asked someone to pass on a message that he'd gone to the show, but they'd forgotten. I wasn't too worried. After all, my Ben had survived a year in the jungles of Vietnam, fighting for his life. It seemed absurd that something could have happened to him at home.'

That seemed the most tragic aspect of this story. For a soldier to have survived such tough odds in the national service and then be murdered at home. It somehow made it even more wasteful and tragic.

'And you found out on the Tuesday?'

Mrs Hayes nodded, tears glistening in her eyes. 'Peter Roberts, the police sergeant came knocking on my door. According to him, the footy secretary had discovered Ben's body. He told me he was beaten, but didn't want to tell me any details. He was trying to protect me, but I had to know. I didn't believe it could be my Ben. They had to arrange a viewing at the morgue for me to see him. There is nothing as horrific as seeing your child lying in the morgue, their face unrecognisable from the damage done to them. He looked more like a victim of a car accident than a beating.'

I didn't know how to bring this up, but I had to mention it somehow.

'I read the inquest report. There was the conclusion that there was a drifter responsible. One person.' I screwed up my face in confusion. 'I found that difficult to process.'

'Exactly,' Mrs Hayes said. 'I forced them to lower the sheet, and I saw his torso. I saw the large boot mark on his chest and then he had handprint marks on his neck, a small hand, no bigger than mine.' She lifted her hand up. 'And yet the boot mark was large.' She held her hand apart. 'How could one man with hands that small have such a large boot print? It didn't seem possible.'

'And did you raise that?'

'Of course. I told Sargent Roberts that there was no way that it was one person. He tried to tell me that the drifter was probably wearing boots that were larger than his feet, but that seemed ridiculous. If that was the case, the boot print wouldn't have been so clear.'

I made a mental note to follow up with Sargent Roberts at the station and see what he had to say.

While we were speaking, Millie remained quiet, but it seemed she was troubled. Was there something she knew that her mother didn't? I would have to speak to her separately and find out more.

After I'd walked the two women to their car, I returned to the footy change room. The door was unlocked, and I walked in, the musty smell of dried sweat and turf punching me in the face.

Hooks were dotted on the wood-panelled walls for play-ers to hang their clothes. There were wooden benches that circled the entire room and extra benches with storage underneath in the middle of the room. The room was dark, the narrow windows near the ceiling facing the west and not much sunshine breaking through. I flicked on the lights switch and blinked from the bright light, the peeling paint and chipped wooden benches now visible.

I looked at the floor, imagining Ben's body lying there. What had happened beforehand? How had he fought for his life before someone snuffed it out. It seemed as if the light had muted and the room suddenly looked sinister.

I wondered what the police file contained that the official coronial report didn't list. I needed to get more information and see if Liam would help.

I had just finished typing a draft and was sitting back in my chair, hands behind my neck, enjoying the feeling of a job well done. I'd produced great work. The picture I painted was about Ben as a person, his love for his family, a high school footy star who was one year shy of finishing his engineering degree before his life was tragically cut short, a life that held so much promise.

In the article, Mrs Hayes spoke about the reasons for her tribute. 'I want those that killed him to know that I will never forget. I want people passing by and looking at the flowers to know a life was lost, a life that I will never get back.'

Art walked into the office and took off his straw hat, hanging it on the coatrack, his shirt already damp with sweat.

I unrolled the paper from my typewriter and followed Art into his office. 'I've just finished an article for the next edition.'

Art sat on his chair and put on his glasses, before taking the article from me and reading it. 'Turn on the fan?'

I flipped on the fan and sat on the chair across from Art's desk. He was in his fifties, but looked older. His fair skin was mottled and red from the sun. There was a puckered scar on his cheek. He'd had a melanoma cut out and was now much more careful with the sun.

Art's lips tightened. 'I'm not sure…' He took off his glasses and tapped the table with the temple tip. 'Something is missing.'

'Oh.' I crossed my arms, my earlier feeling of elation beaten down. 'I thought it was a great angle—a local boy mown down in his prime, an unsolved murder, a family torn apart by the tragedy, all tied up neatly with the thirtieth anniversary since his death.'

'Yes, leave it with me and I'll have a think about it and get back to you with more notes.' Art smiled as he took out a brown pill bottle, the tablets clanking as they hit the glass sides. He opened the lid and tossed out a couple of tablets into his hand.

'Okay.' I left Art's office confused. Since beginning my cadetship at the Riverwood Times, he had been nothing but helpful and encouraging. He'd loved all my ideas and supported my articles. This was the first time that I'd ever seen him less than enthusiastic. Perhaps it was the nature of the article. Up until now I'd been writing local flavour pieces that were casting the town of Riverwood in a positive light. This was my first crime story, and one that didn't shine a particularly favourable light on the police force in the town. Maybe Art was being cautious.

The next morning, I eagerly walked to the gorge and to my meeting with Dawn. I had been in a state of nervous excitement, wondering what she wanted to show me.

She was already waiting for me, staring at the tribute. I'd brought my notebook.

'Who is the tribute for?' I asked, after she'd finished praying.

She took the notebook and wrote.

Friend Maureen.

'What happened to Maureen?'

Dawn shrugged.

'Did she drown in the gorge?' I pointed to the undulating waters behind us.

Dawn didn't speak. She handed me the diary she was holding.

Read this. Find Maureen.

I took the diary and opened to the first page.

Ђћек се паркирао испред претуиене ломаие, и отворио врата свог утехе да изаре. Вирио сам кроз прозор. Где смо стали? Предње дворильте је било пуно зарралих љкољки од три аутомобила и разних других моторних делова.

It was neat, cursive handwriting in Cyrillic. When undertaking the schooling system in what was Yugoslavia, before the latest conflict that ended in 1995, the national school system had taught both the Latin alphabet and the Cyrillic alphabet in alternating weeks, ensuring that its citizens were fluent in both. Since the end of the Balkan War, where the countries that were Yugoslavia sought independence, the Cyrillic alphabet became the one that Serbs used, while Croatia and Bosnia reverted to the Latin alphabet. This would have been a foolproof system of writing that would have ensured that no one could read her diary. No Australian could decipher these letters into words.

'Are you sure you want me to read your diary?' I was both honoured and afraid. It seemed like such an invasion of privacy and one that I hadn't earned. After all, we had just met the day before.

Dawn didn't speak, but her eyes spoke for her. There was a lifetime of loneliness and pain. This was a need that couldn't be ignored.

'Alright. I'll read it. Can we meet tomorrow so I can talk to you about it?'

Dawn nodded. She waved for me to go.

'You want me to leave you?'

She nodded.

I returned my notebook and diary to my backpack and left the gorge. As I walked, I turned over my shoulder. Dawn was staring out at the gorge, her shoulders sloped with pain. My skin broke out in goosepimples. What was going on with her?

When I got to the car I wanted to dive into the diary and read, but it would be uncomfortable for Dawn to walk past and see me still parked here, pawing through her belongings. My eyes glanced at the clock. I still had an hour until I was due at work. I could go to the office and read there, but that seemed wrong. Dawn had given me this in the strictest of confidentiality. I didn't want anyone asking me questions as I read.

I turned on the car and did a u-turn. Before going to work, I could go home and read. I couldn't wait to find out. I parked in my driveway and ran up the porch, sitting on the chairs, and opened the diary.

Dawn's diary

1973

Jack parked in front of a beaten weatherboard house and opened the door of his ute to get out. I peered out the window. Where were we? The front yard was littered with the rusted shells of three cars and various other motor parts. There was a stack of rubber tyres beside the house under an elm tree and a pink Holden sedan with a white rooftop parked in the driveway.

My sister-in-law, Patty, appeared on the sagging porch, her plump frame stretching taut over the flower patterned dress she was wearing. She held a pink-cheeked baby in her arms. Jack's brother Harvey came to stand beside her. Jack and Harvey had the same sticky out ears and plain face, but Jack was tall and lanky, while Harvey's frame was broader and he had a slight pot belly. I breathed a sigh of relief. We must be stopping off at Patty and Harvey's house before we made our way home. Jack had told me they had moved to a new house.

I waited by the ute as Jack walked over to the letterbox and lifted the top, taking out a newspaper. I read the title Riverwood Times. He returned to the ute tray and took out my suitcase, carrying it up the stairs. Why was he taking my suitcase into Patty and Harvey's house?

I hesitantly climbed the stairs after him, holding onto the peeling banister, the white paint chipped so badly that it barely covered the wood.

I was climbing the stairs, not able to see my feet from my protruding stomach.

'It's not much,' Jack said as he walked up the stairs in front of me. 'But the rent's cheap and there's plenty of space for me to do some work on the side fixing cars.'

I stopped climbing, the memory fading from my eyes like a mirage, and once again I was in the present with my husband and in-laws on the porch, waiting for me to climb the last step.

'Welcome home. We came over early to get the place ready for you. This one's been living like a bachelor for the past four months, so I came to hide his sins.' Patty nodded at Jack.

'It wasn't that bad!' Jack's cheeks turned pink.

I climbed the last step, and now we all stood on the porch. I heard shrieking children and realised that Patty and Harvey's sons were playing in the backyard.

'I thought you'd be dying to see her.' Patty deftly handed the baby into my arms.

My muscles became rigid as I held the soft bundle. The baby took one look at my bewildered face and revolted, her back arching up as she stiffened, her mouth breaking open like a split apple. I hesitated. Should I hand her back or try to comfort her? If I didn't comfort the baby, there would be one more black mark against me as a negligent mother.

'Come here, baby girl.' Jack gently interjected himself in the mix. He took the baby in his arms, leaning his sandy head to her dark, and she instantly gurgled. They gazed at each other with mutual admiration in their identical brown eyes.

'She's crying because she hasn't seen her mum for a few weeks,' Patty said.

I heard the rebuke in her voice. I had rejected any further visits from the baby, needing to immerse herself in my last few weeks of peace and quiet at the hospital before my return to so called 'normality.'

'She's got another two months,' Harvey said.

Patty sighed heavily. She had been caring for the baby for four months now while I was in the hospital, in between working on the tobacco farm, and she bore dark circles under her eyes. She already had a five-year-old, a toddler, and the baby was just an added burden.

Dr Fox had created a transition plan for me before I left. First, I had to return home for two months and take on my normal duties, while building up what he called 'bonding time' with the baby, before I transitioned back to having my daughter under the same roof.

As Jack held our baby, he gently smiled at me, and I knew he was picturing the three of us under the same roof as the perfect family. But all I felt was relief that I had another two month reprieve.

'Let's go in.' Patty herded us inside.

As I stepped into the hallway, my memory returned, as if a lightswitch was flicked on. Jack and I'd moved into the house after we married. But when I tried to remember how we met or our wedding, I came up blank. I panted as my heart sped up. As I made it through the door, I felt relieved that no one could see me taking deep breaths the way Dr Fox had taught me. I'd told him that my memory was being affected by the treatment. I'd received electric shock therapy three times a week for the first six weeks of my hospitalisation, but I hadn't been completely honest about how much I forgot.

I remembered my childhood in Yugoslavia and migrating to Australia and moving to Riverwood when I was seventeen years old, but when I searched the corners of my mind for memories of the past year, it was like there was a fog hiding it. I'd been too afraid to tell Dr Fox, afraid that he wouldn't let me out of the hospital, and so I'd just prayed that when I came home, the fog would lift.

We stepped into the living room, and memories hit me like flashbulbs. Harvey sat on the low olive green couch that Jack's parents had bought us as a wedding present. Jack sat on the matching armchair and bounced the baby on his knee, making her squeal with glee. I stood awkwardly, unsure whether to sit.

'Would you like a coffee?' Patty asked, nodding at the kitchen.

I flushed, realising that Patty was taking on the role of hostess when this was my house.

'You sit down. I'll make coffee.' I put my handbag down on the top of the television. Jack had bought the latest model, the television screen inlaid in the large square wooden cabinet so that it looked like a distinguished piece of furniture, putting down a payment from his first paycheck. I'd been so excited to put the television out on display, now it was just a reminder of my last moment of sanity. I'd heard voices coming from the television when it was turned off. The screen was a black mirror reflecting my distorted face.

'I'll help.' Patty went to follow me.

'No, no. I insist you sit.' I forced a smile, but my tone brooked no argument. I desperately needed a moment to herself to process my disconnected memories. I was relieved to see that Patty subsided back into the sofa with a sigh.

Even though I hadn't stepped into the kitchen, I knew it had black and white checked linoleum floor and aqua green cabinets. There was a vinyl table and chrome white padded chairs we'd bought. When I crossed through the threshold, I was relieved to see that my memories matched the reality.

I filled the copper kettle that had belonged to Jack's grandmother, who had passed it on as a family heirloom, and placed it on the stovetop. My muscle memory returned, and I instinctively opened the top cupboard next to the kitchen sink and found the coffee pot set, lining up the brown and orange patterned mugs next to the coffeepot, and then the right-hand drawer next to the fridge to find the utensils. Maybe Dr Fox was right. It was just a matter of me settling into my old routine and the swiss cheese memory holes from the treatment would be filled.

I spooned the Nescafe into the coffee pot and added the boiled water from the kettle. I returned with a tray and knelt by the coffee table, serving coffee to Patty and Harvey.

I handed Jack his coffee. He took a sip and scrunched up his face. I'd put sugar in it, but he took it black. I went to take the cup back, but Jack shook his head.

'It's fine.' He took another sip, only the tightening of his lips showing his distaste.

I looked at the braided woollen rug and remembered my mother-in-law made it as a housewarming present, my fingers tracing the black border next to my knees, as tears stung my eyes. What sort of wife didn't know her husband's coffee preferences?

The baby lay on her back, kicking her feet and dribbling as she peered at me. I tickled the baby's foot, making her smile widely. I forced a smile for the baby, grabbing her little feet, relief flowing out of the adults behind me like a cool breeze. I was acting like a normal mother.

Every movement felt like a test.

I'd never been much into babies. As one of the older daughters out of seven siblings I'd spent most of my life helping my mother care for the young ones, and what little maternal affection I'd felt had leaked out with all cloth nappies I'd scrubbed faeces out of.

The baby cried. I waited a beat for Patty to react, but Patty watched me carefully, and I realised that my sister-law-expected me to pick the baby up. I leaned down and scooped the baby up, holding her against my chest. The baby leaned back, trying to look at me. Its hands reached for my face, wanting to trace it. I endured its touch for a moment, before quickly turning her around to look at the other adults.

Half an hour later, I carried the baby as I walked Patty and Harvey out, their two sons running toward the car. I waited by the passenger seat to hand the baby to Patty.

'Do you want to give her a kiss?' Patty asked after she'd buckled her sons into the car.

I nodded, and ducked down and kissed it on the forehead, breathing in the scent of talcum powder.

'Thanks Patty,' I said as I stepped back.

'I'll drop her off in the morning.'

I nodded, waving as the car went down the road.

'I can't wait for when we'll all be under the same roof.' Jack put his arm around my shoulders and we stood on the porch.

I waited a few moments before ducking out from under Jack's arm. 'I'll go wash the dishes.'

'I'll help.'

I heard Jack collecting the cups, saucers and then his tread as he followed me. I made my way to the living room without looking back. Moving to the kitchen, I placed the dishes on the tray. I filled the sink with warm water and put in suds.

'That went well.' Jack grabbed a tea towel.

'Mmm,' I muttered.

'Maybe we won't have to wait two months. Maybe we can begin having Azra stay overnight this weekend.'

'I think it's best that we follow Dr Fox's plan. We'll just take it one day at a time.'

'I guess you're right.'

We washed and dried the dishes in silence.

'I'm going to have a shower before bed,' I said, after wiping down the kitchen counters.

Jack straightened from the kitchen table. 'Great. I put your bags in the bedroom.'

I walked into the bedroom I'd shared with Jack before leaving. I saw he was looking at the bed longingly and the penny dropped. 'I'm really tired. It was a big day.' I yawned for effect.

'Of course.' Jack forced a smile. 'I'll watch television while you get settled and come to bed later.'

I waited until he'd left the bedroom before walking over and closing the door behind him. I unpacked my suitcase and hung my meagre belongings back in the wardrobe. I didn't have much. I'd left my parent's home with only one packed suitcase and had borrowed Patty's dresses while I was pregnant.

When I'd left the hospital everyone was excited for me to go home, but this wasn't home. I'd been imagining the house I'd been living with my parents and siblings, far back on a paddock behind the tobacco farm.

I took my nightie and spare underwear and retreated to the bathroom and had a shower. When I finished and walked down the hallway, I still heard the television. I got into bed and closed the door, lying as close to the edge of the bed as I could. I waited on tenterhooks for Jack to come to bed.

He came half an hour later, gently easing the door open. I heard the rustle of him taking off his clothes and placing them on the chest of drawers, before he eased into bed. He carefully turned on his side, away from me, and while the dip in the bed was pulling me toward him, we didn't touch.

I don't know how much time passed before sleep finally took me under. I awoke to a feeling of choking. There was something sitting on my chest, pushing me down into the mattress. I felt Jack lying on his back next to me, his breathing even as he slept peacefully. Despite my efforts, I couldn't lift the force off, as if my entire body was frozen in a trance. I tried to scream for Jack to help me, but the force held me in its grip like a prisoner. Finally, the presence dissipated and my eyes snapped open. Jack was lying asleep next to me, just like he had been in my dream. The room was as I'd dreamt a moment ago, but now I could move freely. As I moved my leg, Jack murmured in his sleep.

Feeling unsettled, I gently eased out of bed and padded across the floor on my tiptoes. I needed to calm down. While in hospital, I had slept deeply like the proverbial dead, with no recollection of dreams, as the medication I had been prescribed had knocked me out. However, Dr Fox had reduced my dose before discharging me, and now I could dream once more.

As I entered the living room and passed the fireplace, an icy chill struck, making goose pimples break out across my skin. I rubbed my arms as I went to the kitchen and poured a glass of water, sitting at the table and looking through the kitchen window at the elm tree that was bathed in the moonlight. This was my favourite spot to sit. There was something about the tree that calmed me.

'Dawn,' I heard a female voice calling urgently.

I looked behind her, but the living room was empty. My heart sped up. Was it happening again? Was I imagining voices? I took a deep breath in through my nose and breathed out through my mouth, just the way my doctor taught me. My panic dissipated after taking five breaths. I was just tired. I didn't really hear a voice; it was just fatigue.

I finished my water and walked back to the bedroom. As I got into bed, Jack turned toward me and placed his arm around me. I glanced at his face, but he was deeply asleep. I relaxed into his embrace, thankful for his warm and comforting presence. The dream had unsettled me and I was glad to have someone next to me.

4-Audacity

I closed the diary, staring out at the trees before me, feeling like I'd just time-travelled thirty years ago and lived in Dawn's skin. She'd lived in this house. I recognised the description of the kitchen. I had so many questions whirling in my head. When did she move? What happened? Who was Maureen?

I looked at my watch and swore, realising I was late for work. I unlocked my front door and placed the diary on the hall table, before locking it again and running back to the car.

As I drove into town, I struggled with the feeling of discombobulation. I wanted to return to the house, immerse myself in Dawn's life, and find out more. But I had to focus on the here and now.

I speed-walked after I parked the car on the main road and into the office. It was five past nine. No one paid any attention to my momentary tardiness.

I spent the morning typing up articles and, when I bought a coffee, I added another to my order and walked into the police station.

Liam was at his desk, peering at his computer as he typed with two fingers.

'Got you something.' I placed the coffee on his desk.

'You're an angel.' He picked it up and took a sip, sitting back and rubbing his neck.

'I wanted to talk to you about the Hayes.'

Liam grimaced.

'So you're the girl reporter,' a voice growled behind me.

I turned and found the police Station Sargent Peter Roberts behind me, his blue eyes glaring at me from above his white beard. Liam stood to attention suddenly, pushing his chair into the desk behind him with a bang.

'Seka Torlak.' I'd seen him around, but we hadn't officially met. I offered my hand.

Roberts looked down at my hand and back at my face, purposely snubbing me. He was barely taller than me, his chest wide and arms thick, making him look disproportionate. I forced my face into a blank expression. I knew his type. He was a man who demanded his superiority was recognised.

'You're the one who wants to open the Hayes case,' he growled.

'Correct.' I sipped my coffee.

'We won't be opening that case.' Roberts' cheeks flushed, spittle shooting from his mouth as he spat out the words.

'Why?'

'Because that would imply that the police didn't do a good enough job the first time around, and that's simply not true.'

'Is it?' I queried gently, arching a brow.

Roberts jutted forward, thrusting his finger into my face. He was barely a few centimetres taller than me and was arching on his heels so he could attempt to loom over me. 'It's best if you don't stick your nose in official police business.'

He waited for a reaction. I took another sip of my coffee.

'Martin, get back to work!' Roberts barked.

'Yes, sir.' Liam sat back at his computer and continued typing.

I walked out of the police station. When I passed the cafe, I ducked into the alley beside it, taking deep breaths as my hands trembled, spilling coffee onto the concrete before me. My one survival mechanism from being in a war was the ability to maintain calm under pressure until I was safe. Then the fear and adrenaline surged.

What the fuck was that about? Roberts sure was aggressive and not wanting to open the case. Such a prick.

I walked back to my office and found an email in my inbox from Liam. He'd used to his personal email address.

Sorry I didn't get a chance to give you a heads up.

I didn't reply, my rage simmering deep.

I was working at my desk when Mayor Otis walked past, glaring at me once more. Did I misprint a comma in his column last week and now he was here to complain? He walked into Art's office and the door slammed shut behind him.

I turned my back and determinedly ignored what was going on behind me. I heard Art's office door open again.

'I'm glad you understand how important this situation is to Riverwood as a whole,' Mayor Otis said.

'Of course, of course,' Art said faintly. 'We would do nothing to jeopardise the good reputation of the town.'

Art retreated to his office as the Mayor walked out. I glanced over my shoulder and saw Art looking despondently out the office window.

Later in the day, I took hardcopies for proofing into Art's office and saw my article on Ben Hayes, still in his in-tray, unmarked and with no edits.

'I saw the Station Sargent today, and he told me he refuses to open the case.' I placed the new pages in his in tray.

Art sighed, taking off his glasses. 'Sorry about that. I wasn't sure how to address the politics around that.'

'There are so many police stations that open cold cases now. With new technology and time, there are new opportunities for investigation. I don't understand why he's being so pig-headed.'

'Close the door,' Art said.

After I closed the door, he nodded to the chair across from his desk and I sat. 'The Ben Hayes case was Peter Roberts' first case as a constable. He feels that to open it would be to undermine his initial investigation. He's a man with a fragile ego.'

I received the inference that Art was making. Roberts suffered from Napoleon's syndrome, a short man with an inferiority complex who had to subjugate the world to his will.

'Station Sargent Roberts and the Mayor are best friends,' Art added.

'Was that why Mayor Otis was here?' I demanded.

Art nodded.

'I read your article and it's beautifully written.' Art rifled through the in tray and picked it up, looking at the typed lines. 'We simply can't risk alienating the station sergeant and mayor in a town like this. We rely on the goodwill of our relationship with the police, and I don't have to tell you about the council's advertising budget.'

'Thank you for saying it's good.' I collected it and stood.

'I'm really sorry, Seka. Don't be disheartened by your first story not getting up. You're a talented reporter with a long career ahead of you.'

I nodded wryly and exited. Struggling to concentrate on my other stories, I returned to my desk. The smart thing was to let it go. I was a cadet who needed to finish my hours in order to be a qualified reporter. I didn't need to make enemies and sour my new home.

I imagined having that conversation with Mrs Hayes. Looking into her pain-filled eyes and telling her that trying to get justice for her son was a non-starter because one man's fragile ego was more important.

What I needed was more evidence. Something that would make it hard for Art to turn the other way.

I finished work and went to my car. As I headed down Guru Road, the car motor made a grinding noise and began jerking. 'Fuck!' I slammed the steering wheel. I pulled up on the side of the road, trying to think what to do.

I remembered the mechanic shop attached to a petrol pump. I eased out onto the road, doing a u-turn and trundling back to town and the servo in a backstreet next to the train tracks.

The sign stated Martin Mechanics. I coasted past the petrol pumps and parked in the parking bays to the left of the double doors that opened onto the mechanic shop, smoke billowing from under my bonnet as I pulled up.

As I got out of the car, a man walked towards me, his grey-hair sparse, his navy overalls oil stained, holding a rag in his hands that he wiped his hands on. 'Looks like you've done some damage.'

I slammed the door, hard. 'Yep. Looks like.'

'I'll have a look.' The man went to the bonnet and lifted it up. 'When did you change the oil?' he asked, waiting for the smoke to dissipate.

I shrugged.

'How long have you had the car?'

'Six months.'

'Have you changed the oil in that time?'

I shook my head.

The man smiled, the wrinkles around his eyes deepening. 'I think I know what the problem is.'

'Let me guess—it needs oil.'

The man laughed and continued, 'I need to do a full service and won't get a chance until the morning. Come into the office so I can get your details.'

I followed him inside the building and to a office at the back. He handed me a notepad, and I filled it out with my details. He picked it up and looked at my name. 'Seka. You're the reporter at the Riverwood Times.'

I nodded. Small town.

'I'm Colin Martin.' He gave me a copy of the order. 'You'd best get anything you need from your car before you give me your keys.'

I went to my car and collected my handbag and jacket. As I locked the door and turned, a car passed by, Liam at the wheel in his police uniform. He parked next to me.

'Are you here to apologise?' I demanded, as he got out of his car. I was still smarting at the way he'd left me hanging while Roberts wailed on me.

'No, I—'

'You bloody well owe me an apology,' I growled.

'I know—'

'I'm waiting—'

'I'm sorry. I thought Roberts would approve re-opening the case. He was the Constable in charge.'

'So it's an open secret that his fragile ego is more important than a justice.'

Liam rubbed the back of his neck, looking over his shoulder. 'It's not smart to make enemies in a small town like this.'

'You're the second person to be giving me that advice,' I said dryly. 'I survived my enemies shooting at me for three years. One man's small ego is not cause for concern.' I whirled past Liam and headed to the office.

'I see you know my son,' Colin smiled. I looked behind me and saw Liam approaching. As he came closer, I noted the resemblance between father and son — the same high cheekbones and strong chin; Liam must have gotten his auburn hair and green eyes from his mother.

'I thought I did.' I turned away from Liam, purposely giving him the cold shoulder. 'Can I use your phone to call a taxi?'

'Of course.' Colin placed the landline phone in front of me, it was once white with some black stains on it, its rotary dialler faded.

'Tanner, can you bring Seka's car in?' Colin said.

A large man approached, his hair jet-blag, a bushy beard covering his face. He held out his hand. I realised he wanted the keys and handed them to him.

Anger surging through me, my hand was shaking, and I mis-dialled, increasing my frustration. Liam was hovering behind me. 'I thought you were interested in justice, but you're going to leave a poor mother grieving, never knowing who killed her son.'

'We can try again later in the year—'

'Michelle Hayes doesn't have that kind of time. She wants only one thing—justice for her son before she dies. I thought you understood that was important.'

I slammed the phone in the cradle and turned on Liam. His cheeks were red, his hat in his hand as he started down at the ground.

'I want to help but—'

'You're too scared of your boss and for your future, so that's that.' I took a deep breath. 'Colin, could you please call the taxi company for me? I'll wait by the road.'

I stalked past Liam and out onto the bitumen, standing on the corner of the street where the mechanic shop wasn't visible. All I could see was the large white sign of Martin Mechanics. Even though Art was making the same choice to be cautious, I was more disappointed with Liam. We'd met and there had been an instant friendship connection. We were both close in age in a small town and had spent time together, timing our coffee breaks to catch up. His retreat in the face of adversity felt like a personal betrayal.

A car approached, the window down, Liam peering outside the window.

'I'm sorry. You're right, I'm being a coward. Maybe we can work on the down-low and collect information to force Roberts to reopen the case.'

My rage dampened. He was sincere. 'Good. I was going to do that, anyway.'

Liam let out a bark of laughter. 'I thought so. Get in and I'll drive you home.'

I walked around to the passenger seat and got in. 'I need to get my hands on the police file,' I said, as I put on my seatbelt.

The car jerked as Liam stomped on the pedal. 'I don't think I can get you that kind of help. That would get me fired.'

'I wasn't asking you. I was just thinking aloud.'

Liam eased into the street and sighed. 'You're relentless.'

'That's me. Intrepid girl reporter. So seriously, any way I can get the files?'

'Absolutely not.' He drove in silence. 'But you can access the Coroner's file.'

'Didn't I already get that?' I reached into my bag and took out the coronial report.

Liam shook his head. 'No, you can apply to the courthouse and get the actual file. There might be more information there to get you going.'

'You're not just a pretty face.' I smiled at him.

He laughed again. 'I have some other qualities.'

I sat back, relieved to have another lead. There was hope yet that I would get to the bottom of what happened to Ben. I kept seeing Michelle Hayes' pain-filled eyes haunting me. My mother's brown eyes replaced her blue eyes. I traced a heart on the passenger window. I wondered what Mama was doing? I hadn't spoken to her in two weeks, not since I moved to Riverwood.

'Seka...' Liam called my name.

'Sorry. What were you saying?'

'Are you okay?' He turned into my driveway.

'Just thinking about mothers. Was feeling relieved I had a new lead for Michelle, and then thought about my mother.'

He waited, looking at me with concern.

'We haven't spoken since I came to Riverwood. When she found out about me and Ninu, she gave me an ultimatum: either I broke up with Ninu or I had to leave her house. So here I am.'

'Are you going to call her?'

I shook my head. After I'd left, my heart turned to stone with rancour and anger. I couldn't believe my own mother would turn on me. 'She made her choice. Now she can live with it.'

'Maybe she was trying to protect you. Some parents tell their children hard truths for their own good.'

I pressed my lips together, fighting to retort. 'Thanks for the lift,' I said instead.

Liam nodded.

He waited in front of the house until I'd unlocked my door and waved. After he left, I went to the living room. I caught sight of Dawn's diary on my coffee table. I couldn't wait to immerse myself in someone else's life for a little while.

Dawn's Diary

1973

The next morning I woke alone. Jack's side of the bed was empty, his pillow had an indent and was cold when I touched it. I slowly got out of bed and dressed in jeans and a jumper. As I stepped into the hallway, I heard Jack's voice. When I entered the living room, he was lying on the floor with Azra on his chest.

'There's your mummy,' he said, holding Azra up in the air and turning her to look at me.

'I need coffee.' I skirted around him and entered the kitchen. I heard him talking to Azra in baby talk as he placed her on the baby blanket and followed me.

'Patty dropped her off half an hour ago, but I wanted to let you sleep in a bit.'

I glanced at the clock. Jack was due at Martin Mechanics at 9 am and usually left by now to get to work on time.

'Do you want a coffee?' I filled the kettle and put it onto the stove.

He shook his head. 'Let me show you how to make Azra's food.' He showed me how to spoon formula into the bottle and add water.

Even though I'd had five younger siblings to care for, I'd never used formula before. My mum had breastfed all of them and when they reached four months old, she had fed them mashed bread and milk, or potatoes. When Azra was born, I had followed my mother's example and breastfed, until I was admitted to hospital two weeks after giving birth and given medication to stop my milk production.

'Patty said that you would need to buy more formula and nappies. Here's some money.' He placed a few notes on the kitchen counter. He ducked out to the laundry and returned wearing his overalls. 'I'm going to work.'

I followed him to the front door. Azra was lying on her back on the floor, her feet kicking in the air as she followed something on the ceiling with her eyes.

'Don't you want me to make breakfast for you?' I asked, trying to delay him.

'I've already eaten.'

I looked at the clean kitchen sink. He must have washed and put away all the dishes.

'How am I going to get to town?' I asked. 'The pram won't last on the unsealed roads.'

We lived ten kilometres away from the town centre of Riverwood and there was no public transport available.

Jack took out car keys and handed them to me.

'How are you going to get to work if I take your car?' I asked.

'That's your car.' Jack nodded to the pink Holden sedan visible through the kitchen window. 'I fixed it up for you after you learned to drive. Don't you remember?'

'Of course.' I nodded, faking a smile. 'I remember now.'

'I bought a car bed and put it in your car.' He unlocked the car and opened the back door, pointing to a baby bed that resembled a hammock with steel hooks making it hang off the back of the passenger car seat, and fold out legs holding it upright.

I nodded again.

He picked up Azra, blowing raspberries on her belly, before handing her to me. 'I'll see you tonight.' He kissed me on the cheek, his raspy beard tickling my skin before walking out the front door.

Azra put her fists into her mouth and chewed on them, drool dripping down her chin. 'Since when can I drive?' I asked the baby. Azra blinked her green eyes before clutching my dark hair.

After Jack left, I sat on the couch for a minute. I'd known for a few months that my memory was affected. Every time Jack visited in hospital I'd felt this sense of wrongness, like he wasn't really someone I knew, but I had assumed that this was because our marriage was so green.

Dr Fox had noted that my memory was being affected by the treatment, but he'd told me that when I returned home to a familiar environment, it would all come back. Instead, my mind was a blank space, with flashes of colour like a rainbow that peaked through the clouds only to be hidden again.

I placed Azra back on the baby blanket and walked down the hall. The main bedroom was on my left and the bathroom on the right. I opened the next door to my left. It was a spare room with a single wrought iron bed, a dark wood wardrobe and boxes stacked against the far wall next to the fireplace. I went back into the hallway and crossed over to the last door.

I had to push it open, a cardboard box scraping against the floor as it was moved out of the way. It was obviously a junk room, full of boxes and spare mechanical parts.

I closed the door and retreated to the kitchen. There was a tray of sausages in the fridge and potatoes in the cupboard for dinner later. First, I was going to town.

I carried Azra to the car, holding the baby with one arm while I shook the seat. It was sturdy enough. My nose wrinkled as I smelt Azra's nappy. I returned to the laundry and changed the nappy, placing the dirty nappy in a pail with bleach to soak. I would have to wash all the day's nappies later that night and hang them out, so I had enough for the next day.

After strapping Azra in, I sat in the driver's seat, my hands fiddling with the keys. The car seat was too far back. I put my hand under the seat and moved it forward. As I looked down at my lap, there was a mirage and I saw my pregnant belly protruding next to the steering wheeling. I must have learnt to drive while I was heavily pregnant, because I didn't learn before I was married.

I put the key in the ignition; the motor thrumming to life. I looked down at the three pedals on the floor. Clutch, brake, accelerator. I moved the steering column gear stick into neutral, then put my foot on the clutch. I held down the clutch and moved the gear stick into first gear. The car lurched, but didn't move otherwise. I gently placed my foot on the accelerator and the car pottered forward. I drove out of the driveway and onto the road slowly, gaining confidence as the car kept. By the time I'd reached the town thirty minutes later, my confidence was restored. Jack was right. I really could drive. Relief loosened my muscles. Dr Fox was right. It was just a matter of time before I remembered the months of my pregnancy. I just had to be patient.

I walked into the supermarket and got a trolley. There was a woman in front of me who placed a folded blanket in the basket and then lay her baby down. Azra! I ran back to the car. Azra was fretting, her cheeks flushed red and her mouth a black hole as she cried in the hot car. I scooped her up and held her against my chest, trembling and shaken. What sort of mother forgets her baby? I walked Azra up and down in the car park until we both calmed down, and afterward, we returned to the supermarket. I hadn't brought a blanket for the trolley, so I carried Azra in my arms as I walked to the baby food aisle. I got the same formula tin Patty used and carried it in my other hand to the register.

At the checkout, I heard whispers behind me. I turned and saw a woman, her postal office badge proclaiming her as Clarence, talking to another woman. 'That's her. Mad Dawn Winter. She was just released from the hospital.'

I twisted back and handed the notes Jack had given me. I collected the plastic bag and practically ran out of the store. Patty had prepared me the last time she visited. She had told her that when I returned home, everyone would know about me. They would know that I went mad and ended up in the hospital.

I drove home, wiping away tears. By the time I got home, I'd calmed myself. Azra was asleep when I took her out of the car seat and placed her in the cot.

I was preparing dinner, placing the potatoes in the oven to bake, when Patsy barrelled into the house.

'Sorry, I'm in a frenzy,' Patsy said as she fanned her red cheeks. 'The boys are in the car and I have to get home and prepare dinner for Harvey.' Azra started gurgling with joy as Patsy picked her up. 'How was she for you?'

'Great,' I said. I'd left her in the cot for most of the day, only picking her up when she cried to change her nappy or feed her.

'I'll drop her off in the morning again when I take Harvey to work and do the school drop off.'

I nodded and walked Patty out, a feeling of relief settling over me. I finally had the house to herself and didn't have to be on sentry duty. When I saw the clock, a yawn escaped me. Jack wouldn't be home for another hour. I would just lie on the couch for a few minutes while the potatoes were baking.

'Wake up Dawn,' someone whispered in my ear.

I woke up with a jerk and looked around me in a panic. The potatoes smelled very roasted, and I was alone. I ran to the oven and took them out. The edges were turning black, but they were still edible. Jack came home as I was cooking the sausages.

I saw him in the outside laundry through the kitchen window, as he took off his oil coated overalls and hung them on a hook, before putting on his jeans. I expected him to enter, but when I looked again, he was using a scouring brush and dishwashing liquid to clean the motor oil from his hands and fingernails.

When he entered, he sat at the table and I served us dinner.

'Do we have tomato sauce?' Jack asked.

I nodded and got up. I got the tomato sauce bottle from the cupboard and handed it to him.

'When did Patsy pick up Azra?'

'A few hours ago. She came by after the school run.'

Jack nodded, his face creased into a frown. 'I was hoping Azra would be here when I got home.'

'Oh,' I said.

'I might go over to Patsy's after we eat. Do you want to come with?' he asked.

'I'm exhausted. I'll probably go to bed early.'

Jack nodded. 'How was your trip into town?' His knife scraped the plate as he cut off the black edges from the potatoes.

'Good. Good. I had no trouble driving and the car seat worked really well. You're a good teacher.'

'I didn't teach you to drive. It was your friend Maureen.'

'Maureen?'

'I went fishing with Harvey and the two of you tore up the side paddock as she gave you a driving lesson. I just booked you in to get your driver's licence. Don't you remember Maureen?'

'Of course.' I forced a smile as panic took hold.

'Maybe you should visit Maureen tomorrow? I'm sure she'd love to see the baby.'

'I will.' I stood and collected the dishes, putting them in the sink.

Jack went to the living room, and I heard the television. I tightened one hand on the kitchen sink and covered my mouth with the other to contain a scream. Who was Maureen?

As I washed the dishes, I saw a reflection in the window of someone behind me. I turned my head, only to see a shadow disappear. 'Jack?' I followed the shadow and entered the hallway. The shadow seemed to dissipate in the spare bedroom above the fireplace. Did I really see what I thought I saw? I approached the brick fireplace. A brick was sticking out. I touched the loose brick. Someone had scraped away the mortar. I lifted the brick and found a packet of cigarettes and a pink lighter.

I heard Jack's footsteps in the hallway as he called my name. I quickly replaced the brick back in the fireplace.

'I'm going to see Azra,' he said from the doorway.

'Of course.' I moved to the window, my hands closing the curtains. There was the shadow of a man standing beside the elm tree in the darkness. I stepped back and screamed.

'What is it?' Jack asked.

'There's a man out there.'

Jack came beside me and peered out.

'He was just there.' I pressed my finger on the glass window above the elm tree.

'Stay here,' Jack commanded.

I watched through the window as Jack climbed the hill and peered around the elm tree. When I saw him returning, I went to the kitchen and waited for him by the back door.

'If there was someone there, they're gone now. Let's go in.' Jack held my shoulders as we walked in.

I looked behind me once again, a shiver moving through my whole body, what my mother called someone walking across my grave.

'Can you go close the curtains in the spare bedroom?' I asked, too scared to go into the room by myself.

'Of course. I'll check all the windows and doors.' He walked around the house and returned to the living room where I was standing, wringing my hands.

'I might stay home tonight,' Jack said. 'I'll just call Patsy and see how Azra is doing.'

I nodded, relief filling me. I returned to the kitchen and finished washing the dishes. The sound of Jack speaking on the telephone in the living room filling me with comfort.

'I'm getting ready for bed,' I said when he finished on the phone.

Jack sat on the couch and switched on the television. 'I'll be there in a few minutes.'

I got ready and lay on the bed, leaving the lamp on. When Jack came in, I turned on my side and listened to him take off his clothes and put on his pyjamas. I was relieved to have his warm body pressed against mine. A few minutes after we lay down, Jack's even breathing filled the silence in the room, while I stared at the ceiling. Who did the cigarettes belong to and what was the shadow that had led me there? If my grandmother was here, she would have told me that this house had a presence, an entity that was trying to communicate with me, but I'd never believed all the superstition that my grandmother talked about.

I didn't even notice that I fell asleep until I felt something pushing me into the bed. I wanted to shout to Jack for help, but I couldn't move or make a sound. I fought with all my might, but the force held me down. Suddenly the force shifted. It lifted me out of my bed and now I was floating above, watching myself and Jack sleeping. The room vibrated around me and I saw myself lying in bed sleeping as bright sunlight flooded the room, my hands covering my protruding stomach. I realised with wonder that I wasn't dreaming, instead, I was revisiting my past.

I drifted back down onto the bed and merged with my sleeping pregnant self. I woke as a sound disrupted my consciousness. I stirred in bed and tried to return to sleep, but my sleep was broken and I got up. When I walked into the kitchen, a red-haired woman was lifting the boiling kettle off the stove.

'Oh good,' she said, as if we were long-lost friends. 'I hoped that if I banged enough, you'd wake. I'm your neighbour, Maureen.' She waved outside the window to a copse of trees. Glancing outside, I peered through the window. When I'd moved in with Jack a few weeks ago, we'd talked about meeting our neighbours, but we never got around to it.

I knew I should be outraged that the woman had entered the house without an invitation, but Maureen's bright smile disarmed me.

'Hello. I'm Dawn.'

'Lovely to meet you.' Maureen took hold of my shoulders and sat me in the vinyl chair. 'Do you take your tea with milk?' she asked.

Sleep still befuddled me. It took me a moment to connect the tea bags dangling from the cups. 'No tea,' I finally said. 'Coffee.'

'Right you are.' Maureen took out the tea bag and spooned in coffee. She poured water from the kettle and brought the cups over to the table. 'I used to sleep too when I was pregnant. It was hard to snatch a few minutes here and there, but it makes such a difference, doesn't it?' Maureen said, without expecting an answer.

I self consciously sipped coffee, trying to clear the fog of sleep. Since my wedding, it felt like I was tired all the time. I just wanted to stay in bed with the covers over my head, but I dutifully played the role of housewife and attempted cleaning and tidying, and making dinner, the whole time feeling like I was an imposter in someone else's life.

'Has the baby been moving much?' Maureen asked. 'When I was at your stage, it wouldn't stop wriggling. I thought I was pregnant with an eel.'

I nodded. The baby was moving all the time, my stomach looking like ripples on the water. Every time the baby moved, I felt revulsion, as if my body was betraying me. How could this be inside me, eating from me like a parasite?

I was thankful that the woman was so talkative. It meant I didn't have to stumble through a fake response attempting to show enthusiasm. The woman posed questions she answered herself.

'God, I'd kill for a fag.' Maureen pushed her red hair away from her face. 'I don't suppose you have a cigarette?'

I nodded shyly. 'I'll be right back.' I retreated to the spare bedroom and lifted the brick I'd discovered was loose in the fireplace. I removed the cigarettes and pink lighter. Soon after I married, I'd lit up, but Jack had frowned. He found women smoking vulgar and insisted I quit. I'd dutifully agreed and stashed my cigarettes out of sight. I returned with the packet and lighter.

'God, you're a lifesaver.' Maureen took the cigarette and leaned forward as I flicked the lighter for her. Maureen inhaled, her whole face taking on a look of ecstasy. 'It's been so long!'

I took a cigarette and lit up. I'd lost the taste for cigarettes as my pregnancy progressed, but I dutifully had one cigarette a day while Jack was out, just to prove a point. No man has the power to control what I can or cannot do. I got the crystal ashtray that we kept for guests and we tapped our ash into it.

'Well anyway, I'd better be off,' Maureen butted out her cigarette and stood. She took her cup back to the sink and rinsed it off. 'You sit,' she said as I went to stand up. 'I'll let myself out. I'll try to come again soon, but sometimes it's hard to break through.' She gazed out the window for a moment, looking lost. She headed through the living room, toward the front door.

I looked behind me as the footsteps faded, but Maureen was gone. I hadn't even heard the front door open and shut.

I heard a car pull up and quickly took the ashtray to the rubbish bin. When I looked down, there was only one cigarette butt in the ashtray. I blinked, confused. We'd both had a cigarette. I quickly rinsed the ashtray in the sink and put it in the cupboard, just as Jack opened the fly screen. 'Here.' He handed me a bundle of bananas. 'I got them in town.'

He'd left last night with his mates and hadn't returned all night. He went to town most nights and returned during the night or in the morning. Each time he'd return with a small treat: a piece of fruit, a lolly or chocolate. I was convinced that my new husband was having an affair and that the treats were his guilty bounty. I knew I should feel jealous, but all I felt was relief. Since our wedding, Jack had attempted an overture on our wedding night and I'd rebuffed him. That was the reason I'd ended up in a shotgun marriage.

'I had a visitor,' I said. 'A woman named Maureen, who said she's our neighbour.'

'I didn't see her when I drove up. She must be from the house behind us.' Jack nodded to the paddock behind us. We lived 30 kilometres out of town and there were three houses, all within a few kilometres. His parent's house, the house we lived in which was usually given to sharecrop farmers that worked at his parent's farm, and another house that was a rental by a couple that had moved from town. Even if I'd walked, it would take me at least 15 minutes.

I wanted to ask him what he did in town and hear his excuse, but I knew better. A wife did not question her husband. It was her job to accept.

The next morning, I woke up and blinked sleepily as I stared at the ceiling. I looked at the empty bed beside me. Jack had woken up before me again. I heard him speaking and jumped out of bed, quickly dressing. I'd visit Maureen today.

6-Footprint

I lay the diary on my chest, processing what I'd read about Dawn's life. It was hard to read about her struggle with motherhood and acclimating to being a mental health patient in a small town where everyone knew her business.

The attitude of the residents was like what happened in Yugoslavia, before the war, to those who were different. Society shunned anyone with ailments or mental illness. A lot of them were surrendered to institutions to be kept out of sight from regular citizens. A few family members refused and cared for their family members themselves, but these were few and far between. Everyone knew these people and knew to avoid them. They became outcasts by association.

I looked longingly at the diary, wanting to read it all, but fatigue was wearing me at the edges. Not to mention my to do list for tomorrow. I dutifully returned the diary to the coffee table and ate the leftovers Ninu's mother had prepared and then got ready for bed.

The next morning, I collected my handbag and headed for the door, walking the two blocks to the courthouse.

I approached the courthouse clerk, showing her my media credentials. 'Art sent me over. We're working with the police on writing articles about a cold case and he wanted to see if I could get a copy of the file.'

She glanced at my badge, noting the Riverwood Times logo, and nodded. 'Fill out this form.'

After I handed it to her, she took it.

'Art was wondering when he could get that?' I smiled. 'We've got a deadline, and he was hoping to include it in next week's issue.'

The woman looked at her watch. 'An hour.'

I smiled with relief. 'Great. I'll come back after lunch.'

I bought a sandwich at the cafe and turned around to find Mayor Otis behind me.

'Seka, how are you today?' he asked.

'Good.' I nodded, my hands suddenly sweaty. He couldn't know what I was doing here, could he? 'Just getting some lunch.' I held up my white paper bag.

'How are you enjoying our small country town?' Otis asked, peering down at me.

'I like it.'

'It must be such a change after the big city.'

'Not really. I grew up in a small town like this.'

'Oh, and where was that?'

'Srebrenica, Bosnia.'

'And where is that?'

'Former Yugoslavia.'

He still looked blank. Few in the country town were familiar with European geography.

'Europe,' I finally said.

'Ah, in Europe. That explains it.' He looked at my complexion. 'I've been told you're Muslim.'

I nodded, internally sighing. Now it was going to come.

'So why don't you wear a hijab?'

'Bosnians don't wear hijabs.'

'Really, how interesting?' I made a show of looking at my watch. 'I'd better get to eating. Don't want to be late.' I waved as I dashed out of the cafe. There was something about him that irritated me. He was so sneering and patronising.

I walked to the park across the street and climbed the rock stairs to a small alcove, just in case the Mayor had an inkling to follow me. Hopefully, the incline would be a disincentive for him to try to find me.

I returned an hour later and collected the file, keeping an eye out for the Mayor. I ducked into the toilet next to reception. I couldn't wait to see what was in it and couldn't risk viewing it at the office or somewhere in public where someone would spot it. In this small town, everyone paid attention to everyone else.

In the file were the coroner's notes. I read them, reflecting on the official report. In his notes, the coroner had listed at least 36 separate injuries from Ben's skull down to his ankles—cuts, bruises, a torn liver and spleen, haemorrhage of the heart—before he bled to death and died from internal bleeding. There were abrasions on his hands and knees, consistent with the victim being dragged. Cuts and bruises to his eyebrow, cheek, chin and the soft tissue under his skull, consistent with being kicked or slammed against a wall. The coroner concluded that the force and frequency of the injuries indicated the victim had been beaten to death by multiple perpetrators. Why did he write in the official report that there was only one perpetrator?

I flipped the page and found black and white photocopies of photos from the crime scene.

Ben was lying on his back, his right leg bent, his face puffy and unrecognisable. There was a pool of blood by his side and a half a footprint imprinted in it.

In the next photo, there were photos of Ben on an examination table, with his clothes removed. Bruises and scrapes colored his skin. Then there was a closeup of Ben's chest. Someone had stomped on his chest so hard they had left the imprint of their shoe sole as a brand on his skin.

In the next photo, there was a boot beside Ben's naked torso. The coroner used his own shoe to identify the size. It was a size 12.

On the next page, the coroner had placed the photo of Ben at the crime scene and on the examination table side by side, measuring the bloody footprint on the floor and the one on Ben's chest. Even with the scale of the photos, it was obvious to see that the two shoe prints were of different sizes and shape.

The coroner had written a note that the police sergeant stated that the bloody footprint was from a police officer or a witness.

Goosepimples broke out on my skin. There was something fishy going on here. The coroner had included notes on the timeline of the body being found. When the witness had notified the police, the first officer on the scene, a Julie Caine, a constable from the Accident Appreciation Squad who was responsible for investigating car crashes, not murders, was the first officer on the scene. She'd peered in, noted the body, but hadn't stepped in. The first person on scene after that was the coroner who took the crime scene photos.

The coroner had asked the witness, the footy secretary, for his boots that he'd taken back, checking the bottom for blood.

So then, if the coroner had excluded the footprints from a witness, and no one else was on the scene, why wasn't this footprint taken as evidence of multiple perpetrators?

The last note by the corner stated, 'do not believe that the perpetrator was a drifter.' Why then had he written a different conclusion in the report?

I needed to see where the coroner was and get his side of the story. I closed the file and put it in my bag before returning to the office.

I entered the coroner's name in the newspaper archives. An obituary notice came up fifteen years before. He was a dead end. I entered Julie Caine. An article about her retirement from the police force two years ago. The newspaper archives listed her as a resident. I got the phone book and scrawled through. She never married and still had the same name. The phone book listed her phone number and address. I looked around me. The office was tiny. Everyone heard every conversation. I couldn't call from here.

I noted the address, remembering passing the street every day on my way to work. She lived three blocks from the newspaper office. It might be worth trying my luck. I got a coffee at the café next door and continued walking north, toward Julie's street. Within ten minutes, I was walking past the sandstone cottage that was listed as her address. There were beautiful roses growing behind the white picket fence. I opened the gate; the hinges squeaking. As I walked up the concrete path, I noticed security cameras under the awnings. This was something I hadn't seen in a country town before. The windows were framed by white metal bars. Julie was very security conscious.

A dog began barking from behind the closed door as I stepped onto the front porch. The door opened, and a shadow appeared behind the fly screen.

'I'm looking for Julie Caine,' I called out over the barking dog.

The fly screen opened and an elderly woman with short white hair looked at me, her green eyes sizing me up, her hand on the collar of a Rottweiler.

'I'm Seka Torlak, from the—'

'Riverwood Times,' Julie finished for me, her voice deep and hoarse. 'How can I help you?'

'I'm writing an article about Ben Hayes' murder—'

'Why?' Julie cut me off again.

'His mother approached me as it's approaching the 30th anniversary of his death and she wants to reopen it—'

'That won't happen,' Julie said flatly.

'I know. I just had a meeting with Station Sargent Peter Roberts—'

'You'd better come in.' Julie held the door open for me, her tone terse. 'Sit Roscoe,' she commanded, and the dog sat, watching me curiously.

When I entered and stopped in the hallway, she closed the fly screen and the front door, before leading me down to the kitchen, the dog trotting behind us.

'Do you want a cuppa?' she asked, filling a metal kettle with water. The dog sat on a doggie mat beside the stove and, content that I wasn't a danger to his mistress, Roscoe closed his eyes.

'Yes, please.' I sat at the kitchen table and took out the file I'd received from the courthouse.

Julie placed the kettle on the stove and lit the gas burner. After she'd prepared a teapot and cups on the table, she sat across from me.

'I just received a copy of the coroner's report from the courthouse—'

'How did you finagle that?' She lifted a carton from the table and tapped out a cigarette that she offered me. After I shook my head, she placed it in her lips and lit up, the smoke billowing around her.

'I told them that Art wanted a copy.'

'You lied.' She smiled as she placed her lighter on top of the carton.

'Yes.' I paused, feeling off-kilter. 'How did you know?'

'Art is easily intimidated. He would never take on Roberts.'

'He said it was political, but when I looked at the notes from the corner.' I flicked through the pages and handed it to Julie.

'I don't need to look.'

I took the file back.

'I know what the coroner found.'

'You know that there were at least two perpetrators?'

Julie's expression didn't change. She continued scrutinising me.

'This is more than an incompetent investigation. Roberts was tampering with evidence. He influenced the coroner to write a false coronial report. Why? What am I missing?'

The kettle whistled from behind Julie. She stood and poured hot water into the teapot.

'Why are you interested?' she asked as she sat back down. 'You're dead in the water. You have no newspaper to publish an article in.'

'I have a dying mother who needs justice and I want to give it to her.'

'How? By lying to her, too. Art won't publish this article.'

'Then I'll get someone else to publish it.'

'Someone else?' Julie looked at me sceptically.

'Yes. I'll get it published in another newspaper.'

Julie took another puff of her cigarette. 'I tell you what, you get an article published about Ben Hayes in a newspaper and come back, and I'll tell you whatever you want to know.'

'But you won't tell me now?' I demanded, frustrated as put the file back in my handbag.

'You haven't earnt it,' Julie said.

'Who are you to talk? You were a police officer for thirty years and you never did anything.' I stood.

Julie made a bark of laughter that ended in a tortured cough. 'Sit down, sit down girly! You haven't had your tea yet.'

I hesitated, wanting to stomp off and show her she couldn't bully me, but I needed her. She said she would talk, apparently when I earnt it. I sat huffing as I did so.

She poured tea in my cup as I watched in sullen silence, determined not to speak first.

'Milk?' she asked, holding up the milk jug.

I nodded.

'Sugar?'

I nodded again.

'One lump?'

I didn't respond.

'Two lumps?'

I nodded.

Julie poured herself tea, adding milk and three sugars. She lifted her saucer and sipped daintily from her cup. 'You haven't been in Riverwood for long?'

I shook my head, following her cue and picking up my cup and sipping.

'There's some lovely walking paths in town.' Julie placed her cup on the saucer with a snap. 'Especially at night.' She collected a biscuit.

Why the fuck was she playing tourist guide? I was here to get information about a case, not to get a tour guide of the map.

'Particularly the path that follows the Guru River and then past the footy club.' Julie gazed me.

Was she trying to give me a hint? Was there something to be found at the footy club?

'But the best time for a walk is very late at night. It might be too perilous a walk for a young girl.'

Was she calling me a coward? Implying that I was too scared to go walking through town late at night.

'I survived a city under siege for three years while snipers were hunting us like game. I can handle a night walk.'

'That-a-girl,' Julie chortled as she slapped her knee.

We finished our tea in silence, and Julie escorted me out, Roscoe snoozing on his mat.

'Best no one knows about our little chat,' she said, scanning the deserted street. 'Next time you come through the back.' She nodded to the alley beside her house.

As soon as I stepped out, she closed the door behind me. I walked back to the newspaper office, befuddled. Julie was warning me to keep my investigation quiet. To not let on, I spoke to her or that I had the file.

She refused to speak until the newspaper article was published. Why? Once it was published, there would be scrutiny on the case. It would be hard to hide.

I was more confused than ever, but there were two things that were clear. One: I needed to get the article about Ben published, stat, and two, I needed to buy runners so I could go walking.

When I returned to my desk, I opened my email. I wrote Alyssa's email address and attached the file.

Can't publish. Internal politics. Can you do something with this?

I looked at Art in his office behind me. As he spoke to Karen, a smile spread across his face. He saw me looking and smiled at me. He was going to be awfully disappointed in me.

Dawn's Diary

1973

After Jack left for work, I put Azra in the pram and pushed it down the dirt road, determined to walk around the neighbourhood and find Maureen. The first house I went to an old man opened the door. The paint was peeling on the weatherboard, but the garden was immaculate, with neat hedges and pruned rose bushes.

'I'm Dawn Winter from the white house down the road. I'm wondering if Maureen lives here?' I asked when the old man opened the door.

'Maureen?' the man repeated, his face scrunching up. 'There's no Maureen here.' He introduced himself as James Smith.

'Do you know if there's a Maureen anywhere in this neighbourhood? I've just been released from the hospital and I can't remember where Maureen's house is located,' I said, rocking Azra in the pram as I spoke.

'I don't remember any Maureen living around here.' The old man stepped out of his doorway and stood on the porch with me. An older woman came to the door, drying her hands on a tea towel. James introduced his wife, Lydia. 'Do you know if there's a Maureen around here?' he asked her.

'No, I don't know a Maureen that lives around here, but I can ask around for you love,' Lydia said.

'Thank you. I live over there.' I pointed down the hill where my roof was visible.

I returned home feeling dispirited. I'd thought Maureen was in one of the neighbouring houses. She'd always come and gone so quickly, popping in for a few minutes at a time and never staying for an extended visit.

I changed Azra's nappy and put her in her cot to sleep. I lay down on the bed and watched her in the cot. Azra gurgled happily as she lay on her back, sounding as if she were talking to the empty space above her. My eyes drifted closed. The force pushed me into the bed and this time I wasn't afraid and I didn't struggle. Instead, I let it direct my memories.

I was five months pregnant and outside collecting the washing when I heard Maureen calling. I shouted, 'I'm outside!' expecting Maureen to come and be with me while I was outside, but she was nowhere to be seen.

I opened the backdoor, and took in the full washing basket, struggling to get my girth and the basket of laundry through the door at the same. I heard Maureen singing Shout by the Isley Brothers. I followed the sound of Maureen's voice and found her in the living room, dancing around to the music in her head.

'My father has this record. He loved to play it all the time.' I upturned my washing on the sofa and started folding.

'I had the record too, but it's gone now,' Maureen said. 'So where's hubby?'

I shrugged. It was six o'clock at night and still a bright summer day. Jack had returned from work, eaten the dinner I prepared, washed himself, dressed and then went straight back out again. He'd spent every night out and came home late, long after I was asleep.

'So where does he go every night?' Maureen asked as she disappeared into the spare bedroom and returned with my cigarettes and lighter.

'I don't know.'

'Have you ever asked?' Maureen put a cigarette in her mouth and inhaled deeply as she lit up.

I shook my head again.

'What do you think he's doing?'

He has a girlfriend on the side; I thought.

'You think he's got a girlfriend,' Maureen said, as if she'd read my mind.

I nodded reluctantly.

'What are you going to do about it? If it was me, I'd follow him and then I'd put a steaming pile of dog shit in a paper bag on her doorstop.'

I laughed. 'Why in a paper bag?'

'So you can light it on fire.'

'Have you ever done it?' I asked.

'Oh, yes. I gave my Year 9 teacher a little present after he failed me in English. I had the best laugh of my life when I hid behind the bushes and watched him stamp the burning bag out, only to end up with dog shit all over his shoe.' Maureen stamped her foot, then scrunched up her face in disgust. She dry heaved as she hopped on one foot, cussing and screaming.

I laughed so hard I bent over, holding my stomach.

'Of course he saw me because he heard me laughing and I got expelled. And being home so much wasn't a great idea.' Her face darkened as if she was remembering something horrible. 'You should follow Jack next time he goes and fix this bloody sheila who won't leave another woman's bloke alone. And then you should give him a little present. A good kick in the family jewels will make him think twice before he dips his dick into another pot,' Maureen mimicked, kneeing in the groin.

I shook my head. 'I couldn't do that, and anyway, there's no point. It's not like either of us chose this.'

'Doesn't matter if you chose it or not. You still need to know where you stand.'

'How can I follow him? I don't know how to drive and even if I did, we have only one car.'

'Easy,' Maureen said, as if she'd been waiting for me to admit my interest. 'You ride your bicycle to the crossroads into town and then just follow him to the harlot's house. Once you know where she is, then we'll figure out what to do to her.'

'I don't have a bike,' I said.

Maureen stopped in surprise. 'Use the one under the house.'

Maureen finished her cigarette and left through the kitchen, but I couldn't stop thinking about what she'd said. The next day, after Jack went to work, I went out to the yard and lifted the door that led under the house. I peered inside and saw a glint of metal. With a sigh, I crawled onto the ground and yanked the bike out. It was a black male bike, with a horizontal crossbar and a wide seat, covered in dirt. I swung my leg over the horizontal bar. My stomach was still small enough that I had some flexibility and could perform the motion without toppling over. I sat on it and pushed off. The chain was stiff and needed to be oiled. I washed the bike and then went through Jack's workshop and found an oiling can. After I oiled the chain I tried riding it again and this time I glided easily.

I left the bike under the carport and returned to the house to wash herself and change my clothes. I prepared dinner and left it on the stovetop, before writing a note for Jack and propping it up on the plate. 'Visiting Maureen. Will be back later.'

I got a scarf and tied it around my head and then rode down the driveway and onto the road, enjoying the cool breeze pushing me along and making it easier to peddle. I saw Jack's white ute heading toward me, the unsealed road churning up dirt around him. I got off the bike and stood off the side of the road, my face turned away from his car. Jack wouldn't even notice me. He would just assume I was a bicyclist who was avoiding a mouthful of dirt. After he passed, I continued riding. I reached the crossroads into town and bid behind the bushes. Fifteen minutes later, Jack's ute drove up. I waited until he passed and then followed. I figured even if I lost him in town, I could ride up and down until I spotted his car.

I didn't have to follow him far. He stopped and parked on the main road and entered a shop. I carefully got off the bike and propped it against a lamppost. My heart skipped a beat as I saw the sign on the shop's front window. Totalisator Agency Board. It was the legalised betting shop, or TAB. I plodded to the shop and peered in through the glass window, ready to jump back if Jack was looking in my direction, but I needn't have worried. Jack stood at a table with other men, cigarette clouds surrounding them like a mist, and they were all listening to the radio intently. Something happened and some of them groaned, while a few of them whooped with joy. Jack shook his head with disappointment and scrunched up the papers in front of him, throwing them in the rubbish bin.

I had seen enough. My husband was a gambler. I found my bike and returned home, soaked with sweat and my muscles sore, but at least I was relieved some of my rage had burned off.

Maureen didn't visit for a few days. I had just thought I'd said something to offend or make her angry when I returned from the bathroom and jumped back, startled to find Maureen sitting at the kitchen table like she'd never left.

'You scared me.' I held my hand to my chest.

'Sorry darl.' Maureen tapped her cigarette on the ashtray.

I looked from the cigarette to the ashtray with surprise. How had Maureen come inside and light up a cigarette in the time it took me to walk from one room to the next?

'So did you find the dirty Sheila who's been poaching your man?'

I shook my head. 'It's not woman.' I'd followed Jack in the a few times since to make sure and he always went to the same shopfront. I had gone through his pockets and had found proof of his predilection. I opened the kitchen cupboard and took out the empty biscuit tin I'd hidden on the top shelf. 'Here.' I held out the papers I'd collected.

Maureen looked at the paper. 'Shit, you've got it worse than I thought. Your rival has four legs and you'll never be able to win him back.' Maureen rifled through all the papers, looking at the amounts that Jack had bet. 'Judging from these bets, he's a bloody bad gambler.'

I had already concluded as much, and it was reassuring and terrifying that Maureen was on the same page.

'What are you going to do?' Maureen asked.

'What can I do?' I gestured to my stomach. The gold wedding band tied my fate to Jack's, leaving me trapped.

'You might be trapped for now, but you can start making plans so that when the time comes, you can leave.'

'What plans? I have nothing and no one to turn to.'

'That's not true. You have me. And you can make plans. Start a saving tin.' Maureen tapped the biscuit tin. 'Put aside a few dollars from your housekeeping money every week. And you should probably learn to drive.'

I nodded. It was sound advice, and I was going to take it. I would ask Jack to teach me to drive as soon as he came home.

'I'd better get going,' Maureen butted out her cigarette. 'Listen, it's getting harder for me to come through, and I might not be back for a while.'

'What do you mean you won't be back for a while?' I asked. Maureen was my only friend in Riverwood. While my social circle comprised Jack's extended family and friends, there was no one else I could speak to.

'You should probably get that?' Maureen cocked her ear to one side as if she'd heard something.

'Get what?' I asked. There was a knock on the front door and I turned toward the sound. When I turned back, Maureen was gone.

'Dawn, it's me,' I heard Patty calling from the front.

Suddenly a baby started crying, and the house darkened as if the sun covered the clouds. I looked around, my arms raised with goose pimples.

The baby kept crying and crying. 'Would somebody take care of that baby!' I snapped and opened my eyes. I was lying on my bed and Azra was crying in the cot, her arms and legs jerking as her cries built.

I left the bedroom and went to make a bottle of formula. By the time I'd returned, Azra was winding down, her cheeks red and drool and snot dripping down her face. I picked her up and put the bottle in her mouth. The baby hungrily gulped it down.

I remembered my dream and wondered if my memories were real. After Azra ate, I changed her nappy and returned her to the cot. I took the dirty bottle to the kitchen and opened the cupboard. The biscuit tin was on the top shelf, tucked behind the flour. I took it out and opened it. The tin was full of cash. I took out the money and counted it. I had $200 in the tin. If that part of my dream was true, then so was the rest. My husband was a gambler. I returned the tin back to its hiding place and made dinner.

Later that night, as I sat eating dinner across the table from Jack while Azra played on the baby blanket in the living room, I wondered what else I didn't know about my husband? What other memories were lurking in my subconscious that I had yet to unearth? I couldn't even remember how we met and married, and that wasn't something a wife could ask her own husband.

'Are you okay? You seem subdued?' Jack asked as he cut into his meatloaf.

'I'm okay, just disappointed. I went to visit Maureen today, but I think she's moved.' I moved my food around on the plate, my appetite gone.

'What's her surname? Maybe we can check the telephone directory for her address and phone number?'

'I don't know her surname. I mean, I'm sure that I do, but it seems to be misplaced at the moment because of faulty wiring.' I knocked on my head.

'Don't worry, I'm sure you'll remember. Your memory is returning every day.'

'I don't want to wait.' I stood and tipped the food from my plate into the rubbish bin before throwing it into the sink. 'I want to know now.' I gripped onto the sink, trying to hold my emotions in check.

'Maybe someone in town knows her. You could try asking around.'

My death glare spoke for me.

'Or maybe there's a better way. You could advertise in the newspaper and someone who knows her will definitely see it.'

'That's a great idea.' I spontaneously hugged Jack.

Jack hugged me back, and for a moment, we clung to each other. Soon I felt his breathing change and his eyes lingered on my lips.

'Thank you,' I whispered and let go, feeling conflicted. I wanted him to kiss me, but I also wanted to keep him at a distance. He was a stranger, after all.

'You're welcome.' Jack stepped away and cleared his throat. He took his wallet from his back pocket and took out some notes. 'Here, so you can put in the advertisement tomorrow.

I'm going to spend some time with Azra before I take her back to Patty's.'

'Sure, I'll wash the dishes and be right in.' I was relieved to see him go. I had assumed that my marriage to Jack was a love match and that it was just a matter of time until I started remembering my love for him, but now I knew differently. I had felt trapped in the marriage and had made plans to change that. So why did I marry Jack in the first place? Until I remembered the reason, I would not let my guard down.

8-Hungry

I stomped up the porch stairs, my feet lagging from my demoralising day. As I unlocked the front door and entered, taking off my shoes in the hallway, I saw Dawn's diary on the hall table and brightened. I'd forgotten about it in the rigamarole of investigating Ben's death. After I made dinner, I was going to sit down on the couch and read.

I went to the fridge, on lighter feet, and clanked with saucepans, putting pasta to boil, taking out the container of bolognaise from the freezer I'd prepared on the weekend and warming it on the stove. While it was bubbling, I made a quick salad and heated the garlic bread.

The phone rang just as I was serving myself dinner.

'Seka, Alyssa here. Can you talk?'

'Absolutely.'

I walked through to the living room and looked out the window as I spoke. 'How are things with you?'

'Great. Still writing about the gangland murders. Those bastards never stop.'

I imagined Alyssa as I last saw her, her long black hair tied in a ponytail, her black eyes sparkling. Her father was a Nasho in Vietnam when he met her mother, a local. Alyssa had her father's nose and freckles, and her mother's eyes and dark complexion.

'How are things with Phil?' Alyssa was dating a police officer she'd met while working on the gangland murders. They'd been dating for three months and when he came to my farewell dinner, they were very much in the lovey-dovey stage.

'Good.' She sighed. 'He's really, really good. I think it's working. I just want to be with him all the time. And Ninu?'

'We're still doing the weekend commute.' I felt a pang as I realised I hadn't called him since he left Monday morning. Shouldn't a girlfriend want to be with her boyfriend? Alyssa obviously did. Instead, I was more than happy with our part-time relationship and not having him around during the week while I focused on work.

'What about the job and move?' she asked me.

'I love Riverwood. Just finding the small town politics a bit tiring.'

I'd met Alyssa when I was in Srebrenica, one of the trapped residents under siege by the enemy. Alyssa had been a journalist who came, a window to the world, and throughout the years since she'd become my mentor and friend.

'Yes, I read your article about Ben Hayes. Why won't your editor publish? It seems like the perfect angle for a local newspaper—a cold case, a former serviceman, a grieving mother.'

'That's what I thought, but there's been pushback from the Station Sargent who was the investigating officer. I thought he might cover his own incompetence in the investigation, but I got my hands on the corner's original notes and there was more than one perpetrator.'

'Mmmm,' Alyssa said. 'Sounds like there's more going on there. A lot more under the surface.'

'I spoke to a female police officer who was the first officer at the crime scene. She knows something, but she won't tell me anything until an article is published.

'Oh,' Alyssa said.

My stomach dropped. That didn't sound good.

'That's why I was calling. This is a great local story, but there's just not enough juice for a national newspaper to pick it up.'

'Maybe I can rewrite now that I've got the coronial file. There are so many notes that make little sense.' I told her about the footprints.

'Yes, but you can't use any of it without a corroborating source, and anyway, that just points to police negligence, which wouldn't be a surprise.'

'Julie said something else. Something about the footy club. I think I need to do some more digging and I might have something.'

'Good. Well, if you give me more juice, I will gladly hit publish. Have you thought about your cadetship, though? Art could get his nose bent out of joint.'

'Yes. I've thought about it.' The only reason I was in River-wood was the cadetship. Without it, I had nothing.

'But you're still going to do it?' Alyssa asked.

'I have to. I can't let Michelle Hayes down. She has months to live, and she needs justice.'

'Good. I was just checking. Well, if Art pulls the plug on the cadetship, I've already spoken to my editor and we'll find space for you here.'

'Thanks Alyssa.'

We talked for a few more minutes, exchanging news.

I looked at Dawn's diary, but felt too demoralised to read.

The rest of the week passed in a blur. I came home every night and compiled my notes about Ben's murder, attempting to figure out a new angle. Before I knew it the week was done and it was Friday night.

A red car pulled into my driveway, and I ran down the porch stairs. As Phuong-Vy opened the passenger door, we grabbed each other in a hug. 'I've missed you so much,' I squealed.

'Me too.' She gripped me tightly, her black waist-length hair fluttering in the breeze.

The driver's door opened, and a man in jeans and a shirt exited. 'This is Nhat,' Phuong-Vy gestured toward him.

Nhat approached me and offered his hand, his dark eyes sizing me up.

'Seka Torlak.' We shook hands, his grip warm and firm, without being aggressive.

'I'm so happy to meet you,' he said, in a strong Australian accent confirming he was Australian-born to Vietnamese parents.

'Come in.' I gestured toward the house, putting my arm around Phuong-Vy's shoulders. Nhat opened the boot and took out a small pink suitcase and carry case, carrying them up.

'It's beautiful.' Phuong-Vy eyed the white weatherboard house.

I held the front door open, and she entered, rubbing her arms as goosepimples raised on her skin. 'Are you cold?' I asked.

She nodded her head. She called out to Nhat in Vietnamese. He placed the carry bag and suitcase in the hallway and returned to the car, getting a cardigan. He walked back up and held the cardigan for Phuong-Vy to put her arms into.

I teared up at seeing the loving way he tended to her. Phuong-Vy had a tough time with romance, her last boyfriend turning out to be a dealer and stalker. She'd resisted for so long pairing up with someone from her community, worrying that expectations would constrict and constrain her, but she'd found a good one in Nhat.

I gave them a tour of the house and we returned to the living room. 'Would you like tea or coffee?' I asked.

'Tea for us,' Phuong-Vy said.

I went to the kitchen and boiled the kettle, pouring it over the green tea I'd bought for my visitors. I preferred black tea with milk, but Phuong-Vy was a green tea drinker.

I returned with the kettle and placed it on the coffee table next to the cups, Phuong-Vy and Nhat speaking softly in Vietnamese amongst themselves.

'It's a great little town,' Nhat said, as he sipped his tea. 'We stopped at the real estate office and I checked listings. Very good investment here if you're thinking about buying.'

'I'm not sure if I'll be putting down roots.' I flashed back to my conversation with Alyssa. If I had the article published, Art might give me marching orders.

'Nhat can't turn off his real estate agent instincts,' Phuong-Vy smiled, placing her hand on his thigh.

'How's business in St Albans?' I asked.

'Good. I'm hoping to get my agency open by the end of the year. Phuong-Vy will be my partner and office manager.'

'So a family business, then?' I asked.

Phuong-Vy waved her hand at me and I saw the diamond ring sparkling her ring finger. 'The Lu Real Estate Agency.'

'You're engaged,' I exclaimed, reaching for her hand. The ring was stunning. The band was studded with diamonds, a large, brilliant rock in the middle. 'Wow, this is quite a ring.'

'Only the best for my queen.' Nhat reached for her hand and kissed it, while she watched him lovingly.

'Congratulations,' I said belatedly, stilling the words of warning on my tongue.

Afterwards, I walked Nhat out with Phuong-Vy and left them to say their goodbyes. Ten minutes later, Phuong-Vy entered the house, her cheeks rosy and her eyes sparkling.

'Had trouble separating yourself,' I teased.

She laughed. 'That man gets me heated.' She fanned her face.

'Oh, la, la. Is he good between the sheets?' I asked.

'I don't know. We're waiting for marriage.' Her cheeks flushed as she looked down shyly.

'So that's the hurry, then. Maybe you should test that the chemistry between you works before you make such a big commitment.' I had vowed that I wouldn't wait again. I'd remained chaste during the war because of necessity, the worry about pregnancy and birth in a war zone dampening my desire with Ramo. Once I came to Australia, I'd been determined to live, and enjoy everything, including desire, bolstered by the contraceptive pill to protect me.

She shook her head. 'I've waited this long. I'm not going to compromise my values.'

'What do you know about each other? I'm worried you're rushing in.' We sat on the couch and I tucked the blanket around us.

'I know I've made some questionable choices, like Tom, but Nhat is different. We're from the same community. Our grandparents lived in the same village together.' Phuong-Vy sipped her tea, looking pensive.

'How do you know he's in it for the right reasons?' Phuong-Vy was too trusting in the past and I couldn't help my concern.

'He's Australian born. He doesn't need me for a visa. The only reason he wants to marry me is for love.'

Phuong-Vy spoke with certainty, but my unease still prodded me to question her. 'How can you be sure?' I thought about Ninu. The only reason he was with me was because of love. Was that enough?

'I can't, but I have to trust in us. He's had girlfriends who were Anglo. He was burnt, too. We're both ready for commitment and to share our lives with someone with the same values. He comes from a big family and as do I. We want at least three children. We're mature. It's time to get started.' Phuong-Vy was older than me, turning 30 and more aware of her biological clock. While I wanted children, there was no rush or desperate imperative.

I wanted to be happy for her, but I was still full of misgivings. 'Aren't you worried though about being a part of the community? You were fighting to be an individual, to forge your own path.' We had bonded over the fact that we struggled with our community's expectations in terms of marriage and behaviour. Now I was feeling betrayed that she was the one compromising, and I was being left behind.

'The fight is exhausting. I realised what I was fighting for was superficial. I want to belong and be happy. What about you? Have you spoken to your mother?' Phuong-Vy sipped her tea and watched me searchingly over the rim of the cup.

I shook my head. 'Not since I left.' I hadn't seen my mother since that dark day when she found my pregnancy test in the rubbish bin. My period was late, and I'd bought it to check, my heart palpitating and my palms sweating as I waited for the result.

Ninu and I had been secretly dating for six months and while we'd talked about a future together, it was still too soon. I was twenty-two years old and not in the headspace for a baby. I'd just discovered what I wanted to do with my life—be a journalist and I wanted to dedicate myself to it. Not to mention the fact that my family were vehemently opposed me marrying someone who was not Muslim.

When Mum found the pregnancy test, she'd demanded to know who I was seeing. I'd told her about Ninu reluctantly. As expected, she'd issued an ultimatum—either I broke it off with Ninu, or I left home.

While I wasn't sure whether Ninu and I had a future together, I was absolutely certain that I would not allow my family to dictate my life and choices. Alyssa had helped me transfer my cadetship to Riverwood.

'Does she know where you are?' Phuong-Vy asked.

'No.' Guilt squirmed in my gut. When my mother gave me an ultimatum, I'd moved in with Ninu and not looked back, my pride hurt and wounded.

'Because she called me to ask about you,' Phuong-Vy said.

'Oh, I'm sorry for putting you in the middle of it.' I should have realised that my mother would reach out to my friends. What if she'd also called Alyssa? Embarrassment filled me.

'Don't be sorry. Just call her. She's worried.' Phuong-Vy reached out and patted my hand.

'If she was so worried, she shouldn't have told me to leave.' My voice was full of the simmering rage that I had felt since that day.

Phuong-Vy hesitated and then sighed. 'She didn't expect you to go. She was hoping you would reconsider your relationship with Ninu.'

'I did. I have a good relationship with Ninu.'

'Do you? What about his family? How do they feel about you?' Phuong-Vy asked gently.

I squirmed and looked away. 'We don't need our family's approval. We just need to be in love.'

'Are you?' she continued.

'Am I what?' I knew what she was asking. I just wanted a beat to process.

'Are you in love with Ninu?' she persisted.

'Yes, of course.' I couldn't look her in the eye.

'Because you told me you last spoke to him on Sunday, when he left for the weekend. And it's Friday night. So you haven't spoken to him all week,' she pointed out.

I'd been thinking the same, but would not admit it. 'So?' I shrugged. 'We're not in each other's pockets.'

'Yes, but you're not in each other's thoughts, either. It looks like you've settled into a routine. I'm worried that you've committed to him more out of rebellion than genuine affection. Just before the pregnancy test, you were thinking about breaking it off,' she reminded me.

I fisted my hands, not wanting to remember. 'Yes, and then when I thought I was pregnant, he was amazing. He stepped up. He was there for me, without a thought.'

'I have no doubt that Ninu loves you. I'm wondering whether you love him the same way.' Phuong-Vy tipped her head, examining me.

'I love him,' I said, my voice full of certainty.

'But not the same way that he loves you?'

'Why are you doing this? We're happy.' I could feel tears pricking my eyes. She was hitting too close to, and I was about to break.

'I'm doing this because I'm your friend and because I know you. You drift into situations and then your pride prevents you from backing out. Just promise me you won't be afraid to examine what the relationship is about.' Phuong-Vy patted my hand and sat back.

'Okay, okay. Let's talk about something else. Have you started planning your wedding?' I nodded with relief, glad to change the conversation.

'But of course.' Phuong-Vy rifled through her bag and returned with a binder. 'Here are some ideas.' She opened the pages, and I saw cut outs of wedding dresses.

I was happy for Phuong-Vy. She was moving on in her life, working toward her dreams. Afterwards, as I lay in bed, Phuong-Vy in the spare bedroom down the hall, I wondered what my dreams were. She'd hit the nail on the head about my ambivalence with Ninu. I had thought that our relationship was supposed to conclude before I had to move to River-wood. He wanted a family, and his parents firmly entrenched themselves in their religion and community. While I wanted children, it was always something down the track, far, far away. But the one thing I knew was that I didn't want to raise children in any religion. Having seen the horrors perpetuated in the name of God, and the hypocrisy of those justifying themselves, I did not want religion in my home.

It was a conversation I had avoided with Ninu, assuming we had time. When I had the pregnancy scare, I'd been hor-ror-struck. The thought of a future married to Ninu had filled me with fear. I had seen our future, with his parents playing a tug of war with their grandchild, wanting to indoctrinate them, and my mother wanting the same, while Ninu and I were caught in the middle.

I'd called him, shaking with shock. He'd immediately stepped up, promising to be with me. To always choose me and the baby. He had allayed all my fears. We went to the doctor who did a pregnancy test that came back negative. The home pregnancy test was a false positive, and I'd been so relieved.

When I came home, I found my mother and brother sitting at the dining table, the pregnancy test on a tissue on the dining table.

'Is the father your Christian boyfriend, the Maltese?' Emir sneered.

'You can't marry him, I forbid it,' Mama said. 'No daughter of mine will be married to a Christian.'

'So what am I supposed to do with the baby?' I asked, not wanting to tell them it was a false positive.

'Give it up for adoption. You can stay with Mustafa in Sydney. I can't live with people knowing my daughter fell pregnant by a Christian. You'll ruin us in front of the community.' Mama's face was horror-struck, her hair tucked under a headscarf.

'How could you do this, you slut? All you had to do was keep your legs closed,' Emir scrutinised me with disgust.

'Who are you to talk? You have Christian girlfriends all the time. What if one of them got pregnant?'

'Then she would have to convert to Islam,' he said.

This is what pissed me off about the religion. Men were more readily accepted to marry into another faith, as long as the wife converted, but it was frowned upon for women to do the same because no self-respecting man would give up his religion and culture.

'And if she didn't. What would you do about the baby?' I persisted, knowing he was living a fantasy world.

'That will not happen.' Emir retorted, breaking eye contact.

'I thought it wouldn't happen to me, but here I am.' I'd been taking the pill since we moved to Australia, and yet had forgotten here and there when I was sleeping at Ninu's and thought nothing of it, until now.

'Promise to never see him again and give up the baby, or you will not live under my roof.' Mama hit the table with her hand.

'You would discard your own daughter?' I asked, my voice breaking.

'I will do what I have to do. After what the Christians did to us, I will not have one under my roof.' Mama was resolute.

'Well then, I guess it's time for me to leave.' I went to my bedroom and packed up my clothes and belongings. My mother and brother watched me.

I walked out, going down the street to the phone box where I called Ninu. I never returned home after that. My mother made her choice. She would rather have no daughter than accept me.

I fell asleep, having a dream where a force was pressing down on me, holding me down. I woke up.

Phuong-Vy was in the kitchen, the coffee already done, she was sipping from a mug, staring out the window.

'You have a hungry ghost in the house,' she said.

'What?' I asked, bleary-eyed and tired.

'There is a ghost in this house. A ghost who can't move on.'

'What makes you say that?' I poured myself a cup of coffee.

'I had a sleepless night. The ghost tried to inhabit me. I felt this force holding me down all night.'

I banged the cup too hard on the counter, disconcerted that she was describing the same sensation I had.

'You've felt it too,' she said, eyeing me.

'It's just restless dreams,' I said, goosepimples raising on my arms.

'No, it's more than that. It's a spirit of someone. A woman. She came to me in my dreams. She needs help. A woman with red hair.'

My skin crawled and I looked at her in horror. How could she know? There was no way she could have read Dawn's diary.

'Be careful. There is something unsettled here. There is danger.'

If it was anyone else telling me this, I would scoff, but Phuong-Vy was the most level-headed person I knew. She had experienced hardship and pain, like me. She wasn't prone to histrionics.

'I've called Anh to come and pick me up. I can't stay in this house any more.'

'What? But I thought we would have the day together. I wanted to show you Riverwood and my office.'

'Then let's go now. He will be here at midday and I asked him to meet us at the train station in town.'

I noticed her bag by the door, and she was already dressed. 'Okay. We can eat breakfast at a cafe. I just need to shower and dress.'

I returned from the bedroom ten minutes later and Phuong-Vy was in the driveway, her bag next to the car. She wasn't kidding when she said she didn't want to be in the house.

We walked around town, looking into the op-shops and trinket shops. I took her to the forest, and we walked around the paths. At lunchtime, we returned to the town and Anh was at the train station. We had lunch at the pub and then they left.

I lay on the couch and opened Dawn's diary.

9-Dawn's Diary

I pushed my pram down main road, toward the Riverwood Times. As I passed an alley next to the newspaper office I saw a man smoking. Our eyes met and I recognised him from the asylum where I was a patient.

His eyes widened in horror. He tossed the cigarette onto the ground and ran, the sound of a banging door reverberating in the alley.

I bit my lip, pushing away tears. No one wanted to be associated with a mental patient. I gripped the pram handle tightly, breathing in deeply to calm down, taking pleasure in Azra's gurgling face. When I was sure I'd gotten hold of myself, I continued on my way.

I entered the newspaper office and approached the receptionist.

'I have an advertisement for newspaper,' I said haltingly, over the humming of the printing press, holding out the piece of paper Jack had drafted for me.

The woman took the advertisement from me and read it.

Missing friend. Mrs Dawn Winter is seeking her friend Maureen, last seen on Elgin Street, Riverwood, in December

1972. Maureen is 160 centimetres with red hair and blue eyes. Mrs Winter has returned home and would love a visit from her friend Maureen. If you can help Mrs Winter please contact her care of Riverwood Times.

The woman glanced back at me strangely, before breaking into a fake smile. 'No worries, love,' she spoke slowly, as if she were conversing with a toddler.

She told me the price and I handed my note with a shaking hand. I saw the man enter the office behind the partition. I quickly averted my gaze, not wanting to see the revulsion and panic on his face.

'That will be published in the next edition in a fortnight,' the woman told me.

I nodded, and returned to the car and slowly transferred Azra into the car seat, before folding the pram and placing it in the boot.

As I drove back to the house it seemed as if there was a car following me, dust billowing on the unsealed road behind me. By the time I'd turned into our driveway the car had vanished. I was getting paranoid again.

I took Azra into the house and was putting away my groceries, when I heard footsteps on the back stairs. Only Jack used those steps.

'Did you forget something?' I said, peering through the mesh. My heart sped up as I recognised the man. 'Art, what are you doing here?' I asked.

Art tugged on his tie, looking around uneasily. 'Can we please talk?' he asked.

'Talk.'

He peered at the street behind us. 'Can I please come in?'

I stepped out onto the top stairs, looking at the backyard. 'Where did you park your car?'

He pointed to the copse of trees behind the house. I held the door open, looking away as he passed by me. He was so afraid to be seen with me he'd hidden his car away.

I closed the fly screen behind him and turned back to stacking the dairy products in the fridge. Art stood awkwardly by the back wall.

'I'm sorry. I panicked when I saw you at the newspaper office.'

'I noticed,' I said, crumpling the paper bag I'd taken groceries out of.

'No one can know why I was there,' he said, his voice guttural with pain.

We'd spent three months in hospital together, drawn together by pain and loneliness. My visitors had been few and far between, with Jack and my in-laws coming once every two or three weeks, while Art's mother had been his only visitor, arriving every Sunday with her priest. I'd make myself scarce on those days. After Art's mother left, he was even more despondent and grief-stricken.

During the long stretches of time between visits we'd learnt to hide out on the hospital grounds during visiting hours. We didn't discuss our past or our present. Instead we'd spoken about our dreams, each one trying to top the other with outlandish ideas of what we planned for the future.

I'd planned on living in a small inner-city apartment block like the characters in my favourite TV show *Number 96*, wearing mini skirts, dark eyeliner and exposed midriffs. Art was going to become a investigative journalist, uncovering the dark corners of life and bringing some much needed justice to the world with the power of his words.

'Why didn't you tell me your home was Riverwood?' I asked him abruptly.

'Why didn't you?' he asked.

I'd forgotten about my life with Jack, instead when I spoke about my previous life, I had spoken about Bosnia and living with my family in my homeland.

One day Art held his cigarette to his mouth, his sleeve rolled back and I saw the scars on his wrist. I had seen them before, but hadn't asked.

'Have you ever felt like that?' he had asked, nodding at his wrists.

I shook my head. 'It's harder to try than it is to live.'

'I don't know if that's true. Dying is the easiest thing in the world.' He exhaled. 'In Vietnam I saw life cut down in the second it took for a bullet to penetrate a skull, one moment they were a person, and the next they were transformed into a husk of meat.'

'Not if you're trying to kill yourself.' I exhaled smoke.

'I suppose you know someone who tried to off themselves?' he asked heatedly.

I realised my certainty had raised his ire. Dead silence fell between us as I debated whether to answer his question.

'Hanging is the worst,' I'd said. 'When you hang your tongue juts out and your face is full of pain, while you dance on the end of the rope like you're having the time of your life.'

'Who?' he'd finally asked.

'My father. I was eight years old when I saw him going into the woods with a rope. I knew what he was planning.

He'd tried before. I got my mother and we raced after him. By the time we reached him he was already hanging. In the time it took Mum to climb the rope with the axe his face was becoming blue and he was doing the hangman's dance. Thankfully we cut him down just in time.' I threw my cigarette ground it under my heel. 'Dying is much harder than living.'

'I don't agree. While I was Vietnam I saw many people die. There was a beauty in it. The way that the sudden meeting of death sent a look of shock on their face, and then it transformed into nothing and they just left. When you die you go to a more peaceful place.'

'You don't know that,' I'd said. 'You don't know that where they're going is any more peaceful than this. It could be much, much worse. But I know this world. While it's not pretty, at least I know what I have to look forward to.'

'Maybe it's not more peaceful, but at least there's no more of this... this feeling.'

'My grandmother wouldn't agree with you. She believes a restless spirit in life makes for a restless spirit in death.' I smiled widely, as I hugged his arm. 'So really, you're better off taking your chances and staying here.'

He'd shaken his head and smiled. 'Okay, I'll stick around for a little while longer. Wouldn't want you to be too lonely.'

'Thank you kind sir.' I'd curtsied and laughed.

Later, when we got to know each other better, he told me that he hadn't always yearned for death, but once it took hold of him it was like a sickness. The desire to disappear and offload the misery he carried was like a yearning that could not be quenched. When we met he'd begun collecting his medication again, cheeking it, by moving it with his tongue into the groove of his cheek and then spitting out and hiding it in a plastic bag inside his coat jacket in the wardrobe. He'd given me the medication to throw away, telling me he was determined to stick around.

I had left hospital before him and we hadn't exchanged any contact information. I'd just seen our friendship as one of forged from a certain time and place. And yet now that he was here before me, a feeling bloomed in my chest. The same feeling of love and comfort that I'd felt when we were in hospital together.

'I'm sorry Dawn,' he said. 'You're my only friend. The only person who knows the real me. But you know what these people are like.' He looked down at his feet, the lines on his face deepening with pain. 'If they know about me, I'll never have any peace.'

Who was I to judge? If I'd had a choice, I wouldn't have let anyone know the truth either, but I'd had no choice. My breakdown had been so public, so shocking, that everyone knew about it.

'It's alright,' I said. I flicked on the kettle. 'Sit down.'

Art sat with relief, he took out his packet of cigarettes and held it out to me. When I took out a cigarette he held up the lighter to my cigarette, a habit that had become ingrained from our time together in the hospital.

'I think while I was in hospital I wanted to forget my life in Riverwood.' I tapped my cigarette ash onto the ashtray on the table.

When Jack had left after a visit, Art asked me if he was my brother.

'My husband,' I'd said.

'You didn't tell me you were married,' he'd said, voice coloured by betrayal.

'I forget. I forget a lot of things,' I'd tapped my head.

While Art had been slightly forgetful and fuzzy after shock therapy, the shards of his memory returned quickly. Usually he went to sleep and woke up the next day with his past laid out before him like a lego city that had been built over night.

But for me it was different. Each shock therapy took me backwards, and I forgot more and more. There was even one whole day that I forgot Art. He'd avoided me for two days, until I finally tracked him down in our alcove.

'Why were you placing an advertisement to find Maureen? What happened to her?' he asked

'I can't remember where she lives or her surname. The electric shock did something to my brain and there are a lot of gaps.' I dragged my hands through my dark hair.

'Okay, okay.' Art soothed me. 'I'll help you. I'll make sure your ad gets prime position in the newspaper.'

'Thank you.' I smiled.

'But there's something I need you to do for me. No one knows where I was.' He glanced at me quickly from under his eyelashes. 'Everyone thinks I returned from Vietnam a month ago.'

'You're lucky,' I said. 'Everyone knows about me. Don't worry. I'll keep your secret.' I patted his hand.

A weight left his shoulders and he breathed easier. 'Now, you need tell me everything you can about Maureen.'

'I can't remember much. She has red hair and blue eyes. She's the same age as you and she was my friend.'

'I'd better get back.' Art butted out his cigarette in the ash-tray. 'I'll write up your ad and it will go in the next feature.'

'Thank you.' I squeezed his arm and followed him to the back door.

'Now remember when we see each other next time you need to pretend it's for the first time.'

I nodded.

Art glanced across at the yard toward my neighbours. It was all clear. He ducked out the door and walked quickly to the bushes and back to his car.

I watched him go, with sadness and relief. At least I had one ally, even if I was his dirty secret.

10-Beat

Why was Art in the asylum? It was strange knowing something about my boss that he'd obviously been so ashamed of. He was probably suffering from PTSD after the Vietnam war and had to hide his hospitalisation because of the stigma.

I wondered if I could ask Dawn about why he was there, but it felt like a intrusion of privacy. My reading Dawn's diary was to find Maureen, not to learn my boss's deep, dark secret.

My eyes felt heavy-lidded, and I closed them, drifting to sleep. In my dreams, I was in my living room, watching myself sleep. There was a heaviness on my chest and I attempted pushing it off, but it was a struggle. I jerked awake, gasping for breath, and shakily sat on the couch. My mouth was dry. I reached for the glass of water and gulped it down. Reading the diary too close to my bedtime had planted subliminal messages.

I looked at the clock. It was one o'clock on a Saturday night. I felt energised after my nap. It was time for a walk. I changed into dark clothes and a hoody, putting on my black runners. I took a flashlight and went to the car.

I drove half a kilometre near the footy club and parked my car in the bushes by the side of the road so it wasn't visible.

After locking the car, I walked the rest of the way on foot. It was dark in the country. There were no streetlights to light the road. The moon and the stars hung above me, feeling like I was almost a part of them. Most people would be finding the darkness of nighttime in the country a fearful experience. The night wrapped itself around me and as my eyes adjusted, I could see the path before me. Everything within a few metres away was pitch black. It reminded me of Srebrenica. During the four-year siege we didn't have electricity and nights were the only time when we could walk around without being shot and shelled. I'd learnt to love nights and found safety in the darkness.

I cut through the forest and reached the footy ground. Slowly, I made my way through the forest until I reached the changing room, which was at the track's border. I made my tread light, a skill I'd learnt in my expeditions in Srebrenica, pillaging from nearby deserted villages, searching for food, walking past the enemy sentries as they snored nearby.

When I was close to the changing room, I heard the murmur of voices and then sounds of moaning. I glued myself to the wall. Was I hearing sexual intercourse? I glided next to the wall until I reached the window. It was permanently shuttered open. I stood on tiptoes and peered in. There were two men inside, their shirts off, their pants loose around their waist, one behind the other.

I quickly ducked down from the window. Is this what Julie was trying to tell me? Was Ben at the footy changing room because this was the beat where gay met for anonymous sex? I had to talk to his mother and sister to find out if he was gay. This could be the angle I was looking for. What if he was beaten because he was gay? I came from a culture where being gay was viewed with great prejudice and scorn. While I'd had the chance to meet a few gay people in Australia since I arrived, there was still a lot of stigma and prejudice toward them. I could only imagine the prejudice that existed in the 1970s.

While I was thinking, the two men behind me finished. They murmured to each other and then I heard rustling clothes. I looked around frantically. I was too far from the woods to run and hide. If the men left by the door facing the carpark and walked toward the road, they wouldn't see me on the wall behind the changing room. I stuck closer to the wall and waited. I heard them walking away and waited until the sound of their footsteps had retreated before peering around the corner. They were going in opposite directions. One was heading toward town, and the road where my car was, the other toward the river. I heard a bicycle and saw the man by the river was riding along the river path, before disappearing.

The one who went down the road was long gone, so I walked toward my car, lost in thought, thinking through how to approach Ben's mother, when I had the sensation I wasn't alone. I stopped abruptly, lifting my head, scenting the night to see what had alerted me. I heard a thrashing in the woods to my left, and a man appeared out of the darkness. As he stepped forward, the moon shone directly on his face.

'Hi Liam.' I waved.

'Seka.' He was peering toward the footy changing room, attempting to discern if I'd seen him there.

'So turns out the footy changing room is a gay beat,' I said, addressing the issue. 'And Ben was probably gay.'

Liam deflated.

'Do you think his mother knew?' I asked, still processing how I was going to approach the conversation with her.

'In my experience, parents usually know, even when they pretend they don't.'

'Mmm. Well, I guess that's good. You want to come to my place for a cuppa?' I nodded toward my car, peaking out through the brush.

'I think I dropped my phone.' Liam nodded toward the footy changing room.

'You drove?'

He nodded. 'My car's on the other side of the woods.'

'Come by after you find your phone,' I said.

Liam nodded, his shoulders bowed in defeat.

I had finished preparing tea when I heard his car in the driveway. I went to the porch and followed him into the house, gesturing toward the living room where I'd set up the teapot and cups.

Liam frowned as he looked around.

'What's the matter?' I asked.

'I'm pretty sure I've never been in here, but it seems familiar. Probably because all the houses have a similar layout.'

I nodded.

We sat on the couch and I poured, serving him his tea black with two lumps, the way he'd ordered it at the café a few times.

'I'm won't tell anyone what I saw. What you do under the cover of night is your business.'

Liam loosened with relief. 'Thank you. It's so hard in a small town.'

'Does anyone know?' I asked.

Liam shook his head. 'I mean Dad, kind of. I had a best friend, Rhonda, growing up. Our parents dated on and off when we were younger. We'd spent the day at the gorge. We'd forgotten our swim suits and so had taken our clothes off and swam in our underwear. At some point Rhonda swam over to me and kissed me on the cheek. 'I'm going to marry you,' she told me. I went home and told my father that Rhonda had kissed me. 'And did you like it when she kissed you?' my father had asked, a smile on his face.

'No, it was yuck.'

'One day you won't think a girl's kisses are yucky,' my dad said as he started the shower for me. 'One day you will enjoy kissing a girl.'

'I don't know. I think I might enjoy kissing a boy more.'

My father had knelt down and gripped my arms harshly. 'You can't ever tell anyone that. Ever. That has to be our little secret, okay? It's our secret and you only talk to me about it, buddy. There are men out there who will hurt you for liking boys.' My father hugged me tightly. When he pulled away, I realised that there were tears in my father's eyes.

That was the first time I realised that there might be something wrong with me, that it wasn't normal for a boy to think about other boys and want to kiss them. My father had never talked to me about it again, but he had let me off the footy club at the end of the year and when the boys started teasing me. Instead, he'd taught me to box and taken me to shoot.'

I frowned. 'Like what happened to Ben? Maybe people found out he was gay and that the footy change room was a gay beat.'

'You know that at the time of Ben's death, sodomy was illegal and gay men were regularly arrested. Until 1949, there was a death penalty for being gay. And let's not even talk about what the consequences would have been for Ben as a gay man and a former Nasho.'

'I wonder if Station Sargent Roberts had anything to do with it?'

Liam shook his head. 'He's just a huge homophobe. If he catches even the tiniest glimpse of softness in a man, he pounces. He probably knew it was a hate crime and didn't want to waste police resources investigating it.'

'What if he had some suspects, but is protecting them?'

'That would not surprise me.'

'Art won't publish a story about Ben's death, but I can get it published in the national newspaper if I get confirmation that he was gay. Once it's out there, a witness might come forward, or the public pressure will force the police to open the case. I want to talk to Ben's mum and ask her if Ben was gay, to see if she agrees with me going on the record about it.'

'And if she won't. What will you do then?'

I closed the file. 'Nothing. The only reason I'm pursuing this is to get justice for Ben and closure for his mother. If she would rather no one know about him, then I won't out him.'

Liam smiled. 'Good. It's going to make it harder to rally the troops. You know what people are like around here.' He nodded out the window.

'I know.' When this information hit the town, there would be people who would believe that Ben deserved what he got. Maybe some would even suggest that he was asking for it. After all, he was in a public space, probably performing immoral acts and attempting to corrupt others to his perverted ways. 'But I need to see justice done.'

'Okay, I'll pick you up at 11 am.' Liam stood.

'What?'

'We'll interview Mrs Hayes together.'

'You have a career to protect. Roberts will come down hard on you for disobeying an order.'

'I'm guessing Art won't be too happy with you, either.'

'The difference is, I don't care. I just care that Ben was murdered, and I don't care what I have to do to get him justice.'

'I want justice for Ben Hayes, too. He could be me.' He yawned. 'I'd better get going.'

I walked him to the door.

The next day, Liam parked the car in front of the Hayes house. Ben had grown up on the outskirts of town in a yellow weatherboard house with a wraparound porch, rose bushes dotted around the white picket fence. I noted that the footy stadium was a four kilometre distance from his house.

'Are you ready?' Liam asked me.

I nodded and squared my shoulders.

As I walked up to the Hayes' household, my stomach was twisting itself into knots. I clenched my fists, adrenaline coursing through his veins. I had to take a deep breath to settle myself.

'It's lovely to see both of you,' Millie said, as she opened the door for us.

'Thank you.' Liam moved out of the way and let me walk ahead of him and then followed. We had told the Hayes that he was here in an unofficial capacity until the case was opened and I was leading the interview.

Millie led us into the living room. The room felt closed in with the dark green interlinked square wallpaper. There was a large, dark wooden panelled TV cabinet that took up most of the far wall. Mrs Hayes sat in an armchair, her brown eyes desperate for news.

I sat next to Liam on the yellow three seater couch, a brown throw covering the seat. Millie sat in the matching armchair next to her mother.

'Would you like some tea?' Mrs Hayes asked. On the chess-patterned coffee table, there was a tray with an orange teapot and cups.

'In a moment.' I didn't want to protract their agony. 'As I said over the phone, we have a possible new lead, which could be potentially upsetting.' We'd discussed our approach beforehand and knew we had to flag this. This was a high-risk strategy. There was no telling how the family would take this news.

Millie took her mother's hand, and they waited.

I told them about the footy club being a gay hang and that an anonymous source close to the case had led me there. 'I know these allegations might be upsetting, but I need to know whether this is a genuine the lead or not.'

Mrs Hayes covered her mouth as she listened, her eyes wide with shock.

Millie didn't speak, but I noted her face didn't register surprise. Liam and I looked at each other and I knew he'd noticed too.

'This is, of course, off the record,' I interjected. 'We are just here to appraise you of this new development, but this doesn't mean that this is a genuine lead or that we should be taking it seriously.'

'This is a lie. A terrible lie. This isn't Ben. It's not my Ben.' Mrs Hayes got a handkerchief from her cardigan pocket and dabbed her eyes.

Millie looked from her mother to Liam, her mouth opened as if she wanted to speak, but thought better of it.

'Do you agree, Millie?' Liam asked. 'If this is a genuine lead, this could be the key to discovering what happened to Ben and why. Isn't that what you truly want, regardless of what you find out?'

Mrs Hayes paused, looking at Millie. 'What is it, child?' she asked. 'Do you know something?'

'It's true,' Mollie whispered. 'I'm sorry, Mum. But I have to tell you that when we were little, Ben told me he liked boys.'

'But he was a child. That doesn't matter. Children say things,' Mrs Hayes said.

'Do they just say things, or do they tell the truth before they learn to lie? And does it really matter now? Isn't it more important that we find out what happened to him?' Millie said.

Mrs Hayes crumpled into her seat, holding her handkerchief to her face. Liam looked at me. He nudged his head toward the door, signalling that we should leave. I shouldn't have expected anything. Of course, the family would prefer to keep their ideals intact, even if it was at the expense of justice. After all, what could be worse than a poof?

'I'm sorry Mrs Hayes. I didn't mean to upset you.' I stood and Liam followed suit.

'You're right.' At first, Mrs Hayes' voice was almost inaudible. 'I wish he was breathing. I wish he was here.' Mrs Hayes wiped her eyes, sitting up straighter. 'I don't care about who he liked,' she said resolutely. 'He's my son and I love him, regardless. I want to help find his killers.'

Liam looked at me, his eyes wide with surprise. We sat down again.

'Let me serve you tea,' Millie said, leaning forward and pouring them a cup, while her mother collected herself.

Mrs Hayes took the cup of tea and sipped gently. 'I think I always knew there was something different about my Ben. He always carried this blanket of sadness. Now I know it was his secret.' She closed her eyes and tears seeped out. 'How things might have been different if I had known?'

'Did he ever tell you about any young men?' Liam asked Millie.

'No, he never shared any of that. I think once he knew it was a bad thing to like men, he learnt to hide and pretend that he didn't have those feelings.'

'Were there any young men he was close to? Anyone who could tell us more about this part of his life?' I asked.

'He worked with Jason Marsh and he sometimes mentioned him, but he's moved away to Queensland. And then there was Mark Young, who he saw off and on, but he died of cancer a few years ago,' Millie said.

'We could try contacting Jason via letter.' Liam looked at Julie.

'Perhaps he'll shed some light.'

Liam and I exchanged looks. Now it was his turn to take over. We had decided on a strategy, if the Hayes were open to accepting Ben's dating preferences, then Liam would talk about the clues we found out about his death.

Liam held his teacup, attempting to look natural, but he was tense. 'Mrs Hayes, When Ben died, what were you told about the circumstances of his passing?'

'That he was beaten by a vagrant?'

'Were you told that the police only thought one suspect was involved?' I asked.

Mrs Hayes nodded.

'I have uncovered an autopsy report and based on the evidence that the coroner uncovered, I believe that there were at least two suspects involved.'

'What evidence?' Millie demanded.

'The evidence is very confronting, and I would rather not go into details.' Liam looked at Mrs Hayes with concern.

'Don't hold back because of my sensibilities. Knowing that my only son was beaten to death has destroyed any innocence I had.'

'There was a boot print found at the crime scene, but the corner discovered another boot print. The two boot prints are of different sizes and this, together with Ben's injuries, led the coroner to conclude that there was more than one suspect. Now, if the coroner was still with us, I would follow up with him. But he passed away ten years ago and so all we have is his report.'

'So you think he was beaten to death because someone found out about him preferring the company of men?' Mrs Hayes' face was furrowed as she spoke.

Liam nodded.

'Liam and I have a plan. We suspect that there are people who know what happened to Ben, but that they never came forward. We need to put pressure on them to make them make a mistake, talk to each other, and the truth will come out. I want to publish an article about Ben and the circumstances of his death.'

'Are you suggesting writing about this in the newspaper? Letting everyone know about Ben?' Millie asked, her eyes wide with horror.

'It's the only way we can discover the truth.'

'But it would ruin his legacy. It would ruin his good name.' Millie was shaking her head. 'My mother wouldn't be able to hold her head up in public.'

Mrs Hayes remained silent, but at this her eyes cleared as if she were returning to the present. 'I will never be ashamed of my boy. Never.' She bit her lip as she fought back her emotions. 'I will not let the person responsible walk around with no repercussions while my beautiful Ben is in the ground. I want you to write about this and find the truth. The only thing I want is the truth before I am gone.' Mrs Hayes reached out and took my hand. 'Find the truth for my boy.'

I nodded. 'You have my word. I will do everything I can to find the truth.'

As we got up to leave, Mrs Hayes went to the TV cabinet and took out a photo album and handed it to me. 'Here are all the photos of him.'

'I'll get it back to you as soon as I copy the photos,' I said.

Mrs Hayes nodded. 'I know you will.' She gently cupped Liam's cheek. 'You remind me of him. Something about your eyes reminds me of Ben. You both look like you're carrying the weight of the world on your shoulders.'

Mrs Hayes returned to her armchair. The last glimpse I had of her was staring out the window at her rose bushes. The roses she planted after Ben's passing and that she cut every week to tie to her tribute in the footy club.

11-Fall out

Liam walked me to my door. 'What are you going to do now?' he asked.

'I have a contact at the national newspaper, and I think she'll publish with this new angle.' I unlocked my front door.

'That's risky. Won't Art be angry? He might fire you.'

I shrugged my shoulders. 'It's the price I have to pay.'

'Regardless of whether or not you're in Riverwood after this is out, I'm going to keep digging to find out the truth about Ben.'

He didn't need to say it, but by the grace of god, he could suffer the same fate as Ben.

I nodded, and we said goodbye.

I entered the house and opened my laptop, sentences forming in my head.

Ben Hayes was a young man from a small town. He survived his conscription into National Service for a year, only to return to his hometown of Riverwood and be brutally murdered in the footy changing room.

Ben hid a secret, a secret that he knew could cost him his life. Ben was gay at at a time when being homosexual was an illegal act and could lead to 20 years' imprisonment. As a National Servicemen, he would have been discharged.

He survived the dangerous jungles of Vietnam, where both his own soldiers and the enemy were a mortal danger. He returned to the safety of his own hometown and resumed his life, training to be an engineer, only to be struck down in a vicious hate crime.

Ben Hayes' death was listed as a murder caused by a drifter, and yet the evidence points to multiple perpetrators.

I continued, fleshing out the details of Ben's injuries and his last moments, re-creating the frenzy of a hate crime and the intolerance of that decade.

After I finished writing, I felt euphoric. I emailed Alyssa and waited for a response, hitting refresh on my computer every few seconds.

I made myself dinner, keeping my computer nearby. An alert came through.

'In print tomorrow,' Alyssa wrote back.

I punched my fist in the air. It was going to happen.

I walked into the newspaper office and heads turned.

'Art wants to see you immediately,' the receptionist said.

As I walked past her desk, I saw the national newspaper opened on her desk, a photo of Ben in black and white, his mother Michelle next to the tribute in bright colour.

I'd planned on going to the newsagent and buy myself a copy, but at this rate I wouldn't be able to.

When I approached Art's office, he saw me and stood. 'Please come in,' he gestured, closing the door behind me. He sat back at his desk and took the national newspaper from his drawer. 'I see we've been scooped.'

'You had the opportunity to publish, and you didn't,' I said evenly, stroking my palms down my skirt.

'Indeed. Well, now that the cat's out of the bag, you'll have to promise to do the follow-up articles exclusively with the Riverwood Times.' Art smiled at me.

'What... I mean, is that it?'

'Yes. It's a beautiful article.' He ran his hand down the columns. 'I wish I could have published it here, but...'

Art's door burst open and Sargent Roberts rushed in. 'I hope you're firing this upstart!' He pointed his finger at me. 'That article is a travesty.'

'Because it demonstrates your incompetence!' I stood, squaring my shoulders for battle.

Sargent Roberts' eyes widened with rage, and he stepped forward. 'You are an outsider and you have no place here!' he spat, droplets landing on my cheeks.

I wiped my face, staring him dead in the eye. 'Please continue. I'd love to collect more information for my next article about why the Riverwood Police Department refuses to re-open a murder a case.'

'Now, now, let's all calm down.' Mayor Otis said as he walked in, tapping his cane. His cheeks above his ginger and silver beard lined with deep crevices of pain from his prosthetic leg.

Art's office was suddenly small, dominated by Robert's rage and Otis' malignant benevolence. I looked at Art. His eyes were wide with panic as he glanced between the two men. I was finding it hard to breathe in this small, cramped space, my skin raised in goosepimples as my body screamed danger.

'Excuse me,' I shouted, pushing past Otis and rushing out of the office. As I stepped out of the Riverwood Times office, I hit into Liam. He grabbed my arms to steady me, but I jerked away from him.

I moved away, running to the alley, where I hugged the icy wall, feeling its coolness on my hot cheeks as I practiced my breathing. I hadn't had a panic attack in months and had forgotten how debilitating it was.

'Seka, are you okay?' Liam asked behind me.

I waved him away, breathing slowly. He returned to the top of the alley and stood on the street, blocking me from sight. As my breathing calmed down, I slowly slid down the wall and sat on the ground.

Liam approached and knelt beside me. 'Are you okay?' he asked.

'Yeah, just—'

'A panic attack. I know.'

I quickly glanced at him, saw his eyes full of sympathy.

'Are you ready to go back in?' he asked.

I shook my head. 'I'll wait until they leave.'

He hesitated.

'You go inside. I'll be fine here.' I waved him away.

Liam walked back out of the alley.

'Where did she go?' I heard Roberts demand.

'She walked that way,' Liam said, pointing down the other direction.

'Goddamn girl. She's put us in a pickle with that article.'

'Yes, now we might get some tips that will help solve it. Who knows who saw what and has been holding onto a secret all this time?' Liam added evenly.

I peered through the crevice between the wall and the rubbish bin and saw Robert's face. A flicker of fear blighted his face before he quickly brushed it away.

'Art and Otis will have to deal with her now. Let's go back to our office,' Sargent Roberts said.

I heard their footsteps receding and remained in the alley. I wasn't going back until I was sure that Otis was gone, too. While I closed my eyes, drifting into blackness, the tapping of a cane caught my attention. I looked to the street and saw Otis walking past. I waited another ten minutes before determining that the coast was clear.

I stood, steadying myself on the wall as circulation returned to my legs. After brushing myself down, I returned to the office. My things were in a box on my desk. So it was really happening. I was being fired. My stomach lurched. I knew it was a possibility, but I hadn't expected I would be so devastated by the fact. I had expected more from Art.

Art was on the phone in his office when he saw me. He walked over and picked up the box. 'Get your things,' he urged.

'You're firing me?' I asked, tears seeping from my eyes.

'Let's go.' He picked up my handbag and coat, handing them to me, before holding my elbow and walking me out of the office and toward my car. 'I'm not firing you, but that's just between you and me.' He checked the street before crossing and walking me to my car. 'It's best that you work at home on the next article and not tell anyone about it until we hit print. Bring it to the newspaper office on Thursday night by six p.m. I'll leave the front page empty and we'll typeset it and print it immediately.'

'You're scared someone will leak news of the article and stop the printing.'

Art nodded. 'Roberts and Otis have a lot of loyalty.'

I took my keys out and unlocked the car. Art placed the box in the backseat.

'We need to work smart. Everyone will think that I fired you, so you need to work quietly. Not let anyone know what you're doing. We're going to do this quietly and properly.'

'I can just publish a follow up with the national newspaper.'

Art shook his head. 'I've had enough of being bullied. This town has kept its secrets for long enough. It's time we shake them loose.' He patted my arm. 'You've been a breath of fresh air. You've given me the courage I should have had many decades ago. I will not back down this time.'

I sat in the driver's seat, and Art closed the door behind me. 'Here is my home number and address. Come by every night at seven p.m. Park your car by the river and walk across. I've drawn a map, so no one sees. From now on we only talk face to face where no one can see us.'

I nodded. As I drove away, I watched him in my rearview mirror, smiling with relief. Art was the person I thought he was. He believed in justice and truth. He was going to help me be a champion for justice for Ben and his family.

As I drove down the street, I couldn't help but feel there were eyes on me. I needed to see Julie again, but I couldn't let anyone see me. I drove home and took the box out of the car, feeling relief to be away from the town and away from prying eyes.

I checked a map and saw Julie's house was near the national forest. I could go for a drive through, pretending to hike and cut through to Julie's house. That way, no one would see my car near her house.

I changed into tracksuit pants with a hoody, took my backpack and placed inside it all the files and information I'd collected so far. Art had included a copy of the national article for me and I took it. Hopefully Julie had already read it, but just in case. I jammed a water bottle in the side pocket of the backpack and headed for the car. Hopefully, Julie would be more forthcoming now.

As she'd asked, I came up from the alley and knocked on her back door. She opened it, Roscoe on alert beside her. 'I was waiting for you.' She ushered me in and closed it behind her. Roscoe returned to his mat and snoozed again.

She already had a teapot and cups on the dining table, and turned on the stove and kettle as I sat.

'What do you think?' I asked, tapping on the newspaper she had on the table.

'Good work.' She smiled slightly. 'Very good work.'

'So, will you tell me everything you know?'

'I'll do you one better. Pick up that box on the floor.' She pointed to the left.

I bent and lifted the box onto the table.

'That's for you.' The kettle whistled, and she poured water into the teapot.

I lifted the box and rifled through the files. Julie had collected a copy of all the notes that she took on the case. The files were arranged in manilla folders, beginning with the date that Ben was found. I opened it first and saw Julie's neat notes as she recorded her impressions of the scene. I read them, mentally comparing her notes to the final inquest. 'You suspected immediately that there were multiple assailants?' I asked.

Julie nodded, sipping her tea. 'The state of the body. There were multiple footprints by the body, how Ben was lying on the ground, and that he'd been moved around.'

'Did you say that?'

'Oh, yes, and loudly too,' Julie said wryly. 'But the powers that be were not interested. I was re-assigned and told in no uncertain terms that murder was not my area of expertise, and to focus on traffic accidents.'

'But you didn't stop.' I returned the first manila folder and took out another. They were interviews after the police interviewed Ben's friends and family. 'How did you get these?'

'I went through the files after hours. Transcribed them all by hand for myself.' She smiled wickedly, looking like the cheshire cat.

'So you were running your own investigation?'

Julie's smile faded. 'Not for long. The official line came from the top about a drifter. I knew there was something rotten going on. Roberts closed ranks. Mayor Otis and the Station Sargent had words behind closed doors and suddenly, a drifter was responsible.'

'Mayor Otis? He can't be that old.'

'No, Mayor Otis senior. Yes, the Otis' have been in public office since they settled in Riverwood in the 1900s. A very politically savvy family, that one. Like a octopus, they have many tentacles.'

'Oh, that's interesting.' I knew from Srebrenica how the local council could be a corrupt powerhouse, used by those in power as a wealth generator while pinning down the powerless. Was that what happened here?

'Interesting indeed. Drink your tea before it gets cold.' Julie gestured toward my cup sitting on the table.

I picked it up and quickly gulped it before returning to the table. The next folder was Julie's own notes. There was a brainstorm with conspiracy written in the middle.

Hate crime.

Gay lover.

Multiple perpetrators.

Cover up.

Covering up for whom?

Who has the power to cover up?

Who are they covering up for?

I broke out into goosepimples.

'You think a conspiracy is afoot? That they know who did it and are covering up.' Julie demurely sipped her tea. 'Do you know who Ben's lover was?'

She shook her head.

I closed my eyes, trying to re-live the way the murder would have happened. The attack was frenzied, full of hatred. What had set them off? The shock of finding Ben engaging in a sexual act with another man? Where was the other man? Who was he?

'Do you think that they could be a witness to Ben's death?' Julie nodded.

'Why wasn't he attacked?' I asked. 'If he was there at the same time...'

'Perhaps Ben bore the full brunt of their rage to give him time to run away.' Julie flicked through the folder and showed me a file five years later. 'This was my first murder victim. I could never get him out of my mind. Even though I never met Ben, I felt like I knew him, like I owed him. So every year on the anniversary of his death, I went to the changing rooms. Just checking things out, and in 1974, five years after his death, I found this on the spot where he was murdered. She flicked to a photo of a Navy Blue Enamel Metal Pin Badge for Australian National Servicemen's Association 51 -72 Pin Badge. 'I think it was left by someone who was there that night. Someone who still remembered him every year.'

'You think his lover was also a National Servicemen?'

'It's a theory. He had just returned from service and he would have had to love this person very much to be willing to die for them.'

'Maybe one of the perpetrators was feeling guilty?' I asked.

'Maybe.'

'Did you hand this to the police?'

'By this point, I knew better than to try to stir that hornet's nest.' She rifled to the bottom of the box and took out a small jewellery box. She flicked it open, and the pin was there.

'You kept it?' I gasped.

'There was nothing else to do with it. If I left it where it was, it would have become rubbish or pocketed by someone who didn't understand what it could mean.'

'Did you check Ben's serving records?'

'A member of the public can only receive records for those who are no longer living. Our soldier was still alive at this point.'

'Did you speak to Ben's mother about who he served with?'

'I did. That's what got me booted off the police force.'

'What?'

'Mmm, yes, whoever is at the top of this, their reach is wide.' She pointed at the newspaper and Otis' column.

'Art wants me to write a follow-up article, but he told me I have to be discreet. He's pretending I'm fired, but I'm meeting him tonight at his house tonight. If we take all this—'

'No, no. None of these leave my presence. You can look at them here, now. But you cannot take it. And you cannot ever, ever mention my name in association with this.' She clutched the box, her eyes slightly wild, reminding me of women I had seen in Srebrenica, victims of unspeakable acts by the Serb perpetrators.

'Did something else happen?' I asked. 'Did someone hurt you?' I reached for her arm.

She jerked away. 'You cannot ever mention my name,' she demanded, her voice guttural with urgency.

I held my hands up in surrender. 'I promise I won't mention your name. None of this will come back to you.' I thought I was only dealing with a cold case, but the perpetrators would stop at nothing to keep this secret where it belonged.

'You need to tread carefully, girlie. Art, coward that he is, is right. No one can know that you're working on this.' She took out a photo of Ben's body splayed on the footy change room floor, blood seeping from his mouth and nose, his face bludgeoned and unrecognisable. 'These men are animals. They are determined that this goes to the grave. Don't trust anyone. Not even Art. You don't know where this conspiracy leads.'

She squeezed my hand tightly.

I nodded.

She sighed, suddenly looking tired and old. 'I'm going to watch my game shows. You stay here and write everything you need. But you do not take a piece of paper. I'll check everything before you leave,' she warned, wagging her finger. She walked from the room, Roscoe trotting alongside her, and I heard the television begin.

I spent the next few hours in silence, reading through the files, writing my notes in my notebook, thinking through. Julie's fear gave me pause. She was a private woman. I looked around and noticed the five locks on the back door. I'd noticed a camera on the front porch the first time arrived and the steel bars on the windows, a fire safety hazard. But it seemed she was more afraid of someone coming in than getting out in case of a fire. Something had happened to her. Something terrible that had scared her off Ben's case for twenty-five years. She was insistent about only helping me when the newspaper article was published and there was some protection because information was out in the public, but she was still so wary.

I needed to heed her caution. I would only share the bare minimum with Art. After all, he hadn't actually proven himself an ally. I didn't know if he would keep to his word in publishing a follow up. This could be a ploy to keep me from going to the national newspaper. It would be safer to trust Alyssa to publish a follow up and let Art think I would publish with the Riverwood Times until it was too late.

I opened the last file and found a foolscap sheet of paper, the handwriting squiggly, as if written under great distress.

Assault, 19 January 1974.

Smells: diesel fuel, Deep Heat menthol, cigarette smoke. Description: 180 cm at least. Heavy built. Hands rough—manual labour for a living. Conclusion: Works in manual labour, physically demanding job, suffered injuries.

I wanted to ask her more about it, but if she'd wanted to tell me, she would have. She'd given me access to the box. This was all the information she wanted me to read. I'd dealt with enough victims of trauma not to stir up further wounds. In my book, I transcribed her notes about her assailant. I at least had some details about one perpetrator to include in the article.

True to her word, Julie examined the box carefully when I called her to leave.

'It's best you don't come back here again.' She said as she opened the back door. 'I've given you everything I know. What you do with it is on you now.'

She slammed the door behind me, signalling the last word.

12-Dawn's Diary

I held Azra in my arms, walking up and down the living room to soothe her. Patty had dropped Azra off at seven o'clock in the morning, dark circles under her eyes as she handed over the baby with relief. Azra was hot and feverish as a tooth had erupted from her tender gum, and she hadn't slept the night before, keeping Patty and their household up all night. Since Jack had left for work, I had had no peace. Whenever I placed Azra down, the baby would produce a high-pitched shriek that pierced my eardrums.

I walked to the window and moved the curtain. The newspaper was due to be delivered soon. My nose wrinkled. I took Azra to the laundry and changed her nappy. When I returned, I peered out the window and saw the newspaper on my front porch.

I placed Azra on the blanket on the floor and opened the front door, picking up the newspaper. After I unsnapped the rubber band, I turned the page and there on page 2 was the headline I was seeking. 'Lost Friend.'

Art had expanded on my original advertisement and made it prominent. Maureen, or someone who knew her, would definitely see it. Azra started crying. I lowered the newspaper. A movement across the street caught my eye. I peered into the copse of trees. Was there someone watching my house? Azra's cries became shrill, and I returned to the house. I rocked the fretting baby until my arms ached, and Azra got worn out from carrying.

I walked into the bedroom and gently placed Azra into her cot, patting her back until she was almost asleep, and then tiptoed out of the bedroom.

I returned to the living room and sat on the couch with a sigh of relief. I glanced at the kitchen and the chicken I'd left on the kitchen sink to thaw for dinner, but first I needed a moment. As I lay my head on the back of the sofa, the sunlight streaming through the window glanced off the glass of the photo frame on top of the television, making me squint. I leaned over and picked up the wooden framed photo of me and Jack. I was wearing a pale blue silk sleeveless dress with small white polka dots, fitted around my waist and flaring to my knees, holding a bouquet of white tulips, my arm entwined into Jack who looked so handsome in a grey suit. We looked so young and innocent.

I leaned my head against the coach and yawned, holding the photo to my chest as my eyelids got heavy. As if sinking into the sand, I fell into a deep sleep. I felt the familiar presence pushing down on me, but this time I wasn't afraid. I welcomed the presence in. In my dream, I was sitting on the couch staring at the photo. As my fingers traced the image through the glass, my finger tips disappeared into the frame. I pushed my hand through and suddenly I was in the photo.

I was standing next to Jack in the dress I had only worn once before, the night we met at the Bachelor and Spinster ball.

Harvey was holding the camera. 'And a big smile from the newlyweds,' he said.

I stiffened as Jack put his arm around my waist. I forced a smile, trying to stem my rising panic. What had I done by agreeing to marry a stranger?

The flash of the camera popped and now I was standing next to my sister Merjema, the two of us wearing our new dresses, our dark hair swept up and red lipstick framing our smiles.

Our brother, Besim, was going to an Australian dance, and Merjema had wrangled him into taking us with him.

'Make sure you keep an eye on your sisters,' my father said gruffly, waving his finger in Besim's face. 'You cannot leave them alone for even one moment. You know what these Australians are like.'

'I promise. I'll be with them every minute,' Besim said.

He walked us to the car. Merjem sat in the passenger seat. She was older and always demanded things for herself.

'As soon as we arrive at the ball, you're on your own,' Besim said. 'We'll be leaving for home at midnight, but until then, I don't want to see you.' He took a silver flask out of his pocket and took a sip. Merjem snatched it off him and sipped.

'Give it back,' he demanded, reaching for it.

'Here.' She handed it to me.

I took a swig, wincing at the bitter taste. I passed it back to Besim. By the time we arrived at the town hall where the Bachelor and Spinster ball was being held, we were all relaxed and loose from the whisky.

As soon as we arrived, Besim left us on our own and paired up with a blonde Australian girl. Merjem and I passed by the table where the Country Women's Association was selling tickets. I held out the money while Merjem peered inside at the gyrating couples on the dance floor as the Beatles played.

When I saw Jack for the first time, I didn't look twice. He was a tall lanky man with a plain face and sticky-out ears who hardly spoke. His friend Matt flirted with Merjem and she agreed to his request to dance, the two of them jitterbugging on the dance floor. Jack and I joined them, our dancing more sedentary and awkward, but still fun.

Sometime later in the night, Jack and I went outside and sat on the balustrade beside the stairs and looked at the starry night sky. Jack brought out two cups of alcohol, which tasted sweet after the whisky, the alcohol warming me until I didn't feel the cool chill of the night. When he tilted my head and kissed me, I floated on a cloud. His hands stroked me and there was a languid feeling between my thighs. I wanted to close my eyes and let myself drift away, but I couldn't.

'No, stop.' I pushed him away and took a deep breath.

'I thought you liked it.' Jack watched me as if he wanted to eat me up.

'I did, I do. I just don't want to get pregnant.'

When I was twelve years old, I had told my mother that I didn't want children. Seeing the toll that pregnancy and childrearing had had on her — her once black hair had turned grey by the time she was 30 and her face was sallow and lined from exhaustion—this had seemed the obvious choice to make. I had already figured some things out from overhearing my parents moaning and struggling together during the night, and when my mother told me that the penis went into the vagina, I felt repulsed. My mother told me that if I didn't want children, I had to keep my legs closed. This had seemed a simple enough thing to do, but now, as my lips tingled from Jack's kisses, I wanted more.

'I'd marry you.' Jack reached for her again.

'No, no.' I vehemently shook my head again. 'I don't want to be married or to have children.'

'Why are you at the B&S ball then?'

'It was a party. A chance to dance. Are you here to find a bride?'

Jack nodded and adjusted his pants.

'Shame. If only there was a way, we could have fun without getting pregnant.'

Jack paused. 'Stay here. I'll be right back.'

He ran for the double door. I continued sipping my drink. He reappeared a few minutes later, clutching a small foil packet. 'I have a prophylactic. My friend Matt gave it to me.'

I was stunned speechless. I knew about prophylactics—I'd overhead my mother begging my father to use them, but he refused, saying that he wouldn't feel as much pleasure.

'I'm sorry.' Jack backed up to the door. 'I shouldn't have assumed.'

I rose and approached him. I stood on my tippy-toes and kissed him with all the heat and passion in my body.

'I have a swag in my ute,' he whispered against my lips.

I took his hand, and we walked to the car park, pausing frequently to kiss until I was breathless and weak. My mother had told me about the mechanics and consequences of lying with a man, but she hadn't told me how it would feel. Jack lifted me into the ute tray, and I was in awe of his strength. He opened his swag, and he lay me under him, gently caressing me with his rough hands, his lips pressing soft kisses on my exposed body, stroking the fire within me, until I moaned and writhed under him. I'd thought that my mother moaned and groaned because she had been in pain as my father lay on top of her, but now I realised that she'd been feeling ecstasy.

Jack paused for a moment, fumbling down below as he put on the prophylactic and then he thrust inside. There was a burning pain, and I gasped.

'Are you okay? Do you want me to stop?' Jack asked, holding himself still above me.

The pain eased and now all I felt was this need, this itchiness in my skin that needed to be soothed. I dug my fingers into his back, my hips urging him. He began moving in and out, and I felt the pleasure taking over. Just when it felt like I was on the edge of something, Jack let out a guttural moan and finished.

'I'm sorry,' he whispered against my neck.

I kissed him, all the passion burning within me fused to his lips. He kissed me back, and soon his hands were doing their magic, as were his lips. He fumbled down below and he was inside me again. This time his thrusts were slow and deliberate and I felt a building of ecstasy until it swept over me like a wave of a thousand suns, leaving me limp and floating. Jack kept thrusting and then he moaned again, too.

When I awoke, we were curled together under the swag, the stars the only witness to our passion. Tenderness filled me as I looked at Jack's sleeping face. When I'd first seen him, I'd been struck by his plainness, but now, as he slept with a gentle smile on his lips, he was transformed and almost looked handsome. Now I understood how my mother had fallen for my father, but I didn't want my mother's life. So I slowly eased out of Jack's arms and collected my shoes, carrying them in my hand as I jumped off the back of the ute.

I found Besim and Mejrem waiting by the car.

Jack tracked me down the next day, asked me to go out with him, but I came too close to being tempted and losing my life like my mother had. I told him to find another girl.

Two months later, I realised that my night of pleasure came at a heavy price. My mother found out too when I didn't ask for any sanitary pads and after my father gave me a frightful beating, they wanted to send me to a hospital for unwed mothers. Mejrem had a Australian friend who had been, and she told her that when she gave birth, the nurses held up a sheet to hide the baby and she didn't even know if it was a boy or a girl.

That night, while everyone was asleep, I packed a suitcase and snuck out of my bedroom and walked to Jack's farm. I waited on the porch, shivering in my coat, until dawn when the household stirred behind me and I could knock on the door. Jack greeted me with a smile and proposed as soon as I told him about my predicament.

When he drove us to my parent's house, my parents refused to allow him inside. My father told me I was disinherited for marrying out of the community. Jack and I got married at the Town Hall where we'd met, wearing the dress I'd worn the first time we met.

The memory faded and once again I was standing in the living room, holding the wooden framed photo of me and

Jack. Suddenly, the photo became transparent and drifted away.

Maureen appeared beside me. 'Wake up, Dawn,' she shouted.

I fought through the fog of sleep. I woke up on my sofa, feeling heavy-headed. The living room was shadowed, the sun was in the West and the house was silent. I glanced at the clock. It was 3 o'clock. I had slept for four hours. Something was wrong. I moved, and the photo crashed to the ground, the glass shattering. Azra. I stood, stepping over the glass as I walked to the bedroom. The cot was empty.

Panic swept through me. 'Azra,' I shouted. I searched through the house, lifting furniture, checking under the coach. Where was my baby? I ran to the kitchen and out the back door, screaming my daughter's name as I walked all around the house. I heard a faint mewling sound and followed it, climbing over the tyres that littered the yard resembling mini pyramids. I found Azra on the ground, cradled in a tyre behind the shed. Her face was red and her movements jerky. I picked her up and ran into the house.

I dialled emergency services. 'Please help. Someone took my baby and left her outside. She's limp and lethargic.' After giving my address, I got a bottle and filled it with water, placing the teat in Azra's mouth. Azra sucked, her little hands hugging the bottle.

I picked up the phone again and dialled Jack's work phone number. 'Someone tried to steal Azra,' I told him when they put him on the phone.

'What? Is she okay?'

'I don't know. The paramedics are coming. She looks red and limp. Please come home.'

By the time Jack pulled up in a cloud of dust ten minutes later, I had made a bottle of formula and was feeding Azra.

He ran into the house in a mad panic. 'What happened? Who took her?'

'I woke up, and she was in the backyard. Someone took her out of the cot while I was sleeping and put her in a tyre near the shed.'

We heard the whirring of a siren. Jack went outside and returned with a young blonde paramedic who was carrying a black bag, followed by an older, moustached paramedic.

'Let's see how she's doing,' the moustached paramedic said as he knelt beside me and gently took Azra from my arms.

He placed the baby on the blanket on the floor and took off her clothes, checking the skin on her arms and legs. He took off her nappy. The faeces had dried all around the baby's genitals and her skin was red and irritated.

'She seems to be all right,' the paramedic said. 'Can you get some water to help clean her?' he asked the other paramedic.

'I'll show you the way,' Jack pointed toward the laundry.

When they returned with a basin and cloth, I knelt on the floor and gently cleaned Azra. After I finished, the paramedic handed me a tube of ointment. 'This will help her skin.'

I dabbed the ointment on. I heard another siren and Jack left.

'I think our job here is done. I don't think she needs to go to the hospital. Just keep her hydrated and she'll be right as rain by tomorrow.' The paramedic packed up his bag, and they left.

I picked Azra up and cradled her against my chest, walking to the front window. Jack was in the front yard with two police officers, one female and one male. The female police officer spoke to the paramedics while the male police officer went to the side of the house with Jack.

I sat on the sofa, holding Azra in her arms. Ten minutes later, Jack returned with the two police officers in tow. They introduced themselves. The man was Constable Peter Roberts, the female Julie Caine.

'Mrs Winter, we'd like to take your statement. Can you tell us what happened?' Constable Roberts asked.

As I spoke, Constable Caine wrote in her notebook while Roberts maintained eye contact.

'When you went to sleep, Azra was in her cot and when you woke up she was in the backyard?' Roberts repeated.

Dawn nodded.

'How long were you asleep?'

'I fell asleep around eleven.'

'So four hours?' Roberts said.

Caine scribbled in her notebook.

'Four hours,' Jack repeated, running his oil streaked hands through his hair so that it stood on end. 'How could you leave her alone for that long?'

'I didn't. Her cries wake me up... they would have woken me up. I didn't leave her.' I was crying, inadvertently squeezing Azra tighter, so that she stirred.

'Can you show us where you found Azra?' Roberts asked.

Jack reached out and took Azra, not looking at me. He was judging me as a negligent mother and he was right. What sort of mother didn't wake up for her baby? I walked outside with the police officers on each side of me.

'So you definitely placed her in the cot?' Roberts asked as he looked at the empty tyre, the green grass filling the circle.

'Yes, I definitely placed her in the cot. What? You think I put my baby in the tyre? That I left her here to bake for four hours in the sun?'

'Your husband mentioned you were in hospital?' Roberts asked, turning his hat in his hands.

'Yes, I was,' I whispered, looking from Caine to Roberts. Seeing the scepticism on their faces, I realised they had already concluded their investigation and found a suspect in me. 'Please, you have to believe me. Someone took my baby. Someone left her here.'

'Do you know anyone who would wish you harm?' Roberts asked.

I shook my head, wiping my tears.

Caine closed her notebook.

'We'll continue our investigation and get in touch when we discover something.' Roberts returned his hat on his head and they walked around the corner to the front of the house where their car was parked.

I looked at the elm tree, its leaves whispering to me what I already knew. I would not hear from the police again.

13-Last Entry

That was the last page of the diary. I flipped the empty pages, wondering what happened to Dawn after that.

The next day, I drove to the gorge and waited for her to complete her tribute. When she finished tying fresh flowers, she came to see me.

'I finished your diary,' I told her, holding up the blue note-book.

She nodded, looking out at the shimmering water.

'In the last entry, Azra was found in the backyard and then there's nothing. What happened after that?'

Dawn took the pen and wrote down one word.

Hospital.

'You were admitted back into the hospital?'

She nodded.

'Everyone thought you left your daughter outside, instead of in the cot?'

She took the pen again.

Mad Dawn Winter.

She'd been identified as mad, and her credibility was shot. There was nothing she could say or do that would convince people of her innocence.

'What about Maureen? Did the newspaper hear anything about her?'

Art visited at hospital. No one contacted the newspaper.

'Is that why you stopped speaking? Because no one believed you—about Maureen and about Azra?'

Dawn nodded faintly, a tear seeping from her eye.

'I believe you. I believe you that something happened to Maureen and that someone took your baby?'

Dawn looked at me with incredulity.

'Did you ever feel a presence in the house you lived? Like there was someone there?' I asked. I'd been hesitant to put it into words, but after Phuong-Vy's violent reaction, it didn't seem so outlandish anymore.

Ghost.

I nodded.

Yes. I felt it.

I sat, thinking through how to find out what had happened all those years ago. In the diary, she said she'd had electric shock therapy, that it had affected her memory. But there was a memory that she'd had before that. It might be in her hospital records.

'We need to see your hospital records. There would be notes about your counselling sessions, where you told your psychiatrist about Maureen. There might be some things you don't remember now. Would you feel comfortable for me to read them?'

Dawn smiled, touching the diary.

'Yes, I guess if you trusted me with the diary, you can trust me with this. Under Freedom of Information Laws, any person may view their own medical files. We can either ask them to photocopy them, but that takes months. The other option is that we can make an appointment for you to see your records.'

I paused. Would they allow me, as a reporter, to be in with Dawn?

'I don't know if they will allow me to be there.' I thought about how to overcome the problem.

Daughter.

'You want your daughter to go with you?' I asked.

Dawn gestured toward me and then the word.

'You want me to say that I'm your daughter.'

Dawn nodded.

It would work. We were both brunettes with dark eyes and had the Bosnian round faces. Plus, we would keep talking in Bosnian at the hospital, which would give the appearance of family. If I had to show identification and they saw the different surname, I could just say Torlak was my married name.

'Okay. I'll call today and make an appointment for tomorrow.'

Dawn nodded.

'We'll find out what happened to Maureen.'

But it wasn't enough. I also wanted to find out what happened to Dawn. Who had moved her baby to the backyard? I kept coming back that this happened soon after the advertisement about Maureen was published in the newspaper. Did someone purposely set out to discredit Dawn and stop her search? And if so, there was only one reason why. Maureen was dead and someone was responsible. Someone who didn't want questions asked about her.

'Do you know who rented the house before you and Jack moved in?' I asked Dawn.

She shook her head.

I'll get the rent ledger.

'There was a ledger where people recorded who paid rent?'

She nodded.

'That's perfect.' I could see who lived in the house before Dawn and Jack.

The next day, I collected Dawn from her house. She'd taken special care of her appearance, wearing a green shirt and slacks, a multi-patterned scarf draped around her neck, red lipstick lighting up her mouth and foundation on her face.

She handed me a hardcover book as she got in the car—the rent ledger. I quickly peaked at the pages and saw it was handwritten receipts of rent paid going back to the 1940s. I was renting through a real estate agent in town and paid once a month at the front desk, receiving a paper receipt.

Dawn buckled in and I placed the ledger in my large bag in the backseat of the car, before taking off. As we drove to the city and the hospital, Dawn's hands squeezed tighter and tighter together.

'Are you nervous about going to the hospital?'

She nodded jerkily.

'You haven't been back for a long time?' I stopped at a red traffic light.

She held up both her hands, showing it had been twenty-years.

'That's a long time.' I pushed on the accelerator as the light turned green. 'Today you won't have to read anything yourself. I'll go through the files and if you don't want to know anything, I'll keep it from you.'

I put in a cassette tape of Bosnian music, the folk music filling the car. Dawn smiled faintly as she heard it.

We drove in silence for the nearly two-hour trip. In the hospital, the psychiatrist met with us and led us to a room. There were two bursting manilla folders on the table titled Dženana (Dawn) Winters.

After the doctor left, I sat and opened the folder, while Dawn went to stand by the window and stared out with her back to me.

I started with her first hospitalisation on the 20 January 1970 and the psychiatrist's notes as he interviewed Dawn.

'What happened that night, Dawn?' Dr Fox asked.

'I was home alone again. Jack came home for dinner and left again. He was gone later and later every night. I knew he was gambling in town. A woman screamed for help outside. I went to the backyard, searching for her. But there was no one there. Her screams became louder, and I kept following them. I ended up at the cliff and I heard her from down below. I walked down the path. My stomach began hurting, but I was already halfway down and had to keep going. And then I wet myself and water was everywhere. I was in so much pain, it was like I was being ripped apart. The pain hit, and I twisted my ankle and fell, and then I had to crawl down the path on my side to the bottom. The pain kept growing bigger and bigger.

When I got to the bottom of the gorge, a car appeared at the top of the cliff, the bright headlights lighting up the rocks around the gorge. I tried calling for help, but there was a bang, and the car jerked forward, then a woman screamed. I saw there was another car behind the woman's car; it was trying to push it off the gorge. The woman's car made these grinding noises as she hit her breaks, but slowly the car behind her pushed her off while she screamed for help. The car fell into the gorge and disappeared. I wanted to help her, but I couldn't stand. I was hurting so much.

I tried calling to the men, but they went away. It was just me in the icy silence, with the pain, as it built and built in waves. I screamed and screamed, but no one could hear me. My throat hurt and I couldn't scream anymore. Suddenly, I felt this urge to push. I couldn't stop it. Despite my efforts, I continued to push. I looked down and saw that a baby had come out of me. I picked her up and held her. Hours passed as we lay there. As the blood seeped out of me, a sense of peace washed over me. I knew I was going to die, and I didn't mind, but I didn't want my baby to die. I begged for someone to help me. Someone to help my baby.

And then, as dawn broke across the horizon, Jack appeared at the top of the cliff and he saw us. He came and took the baby away. And I knew I would die, but at least she would survive. And I would join the woman in the gorge and we would be together. But then the paramedics came and here I am.'

Attached was a police report from the Station Sargent on duty.

Jack Winter, Dawn Winter's husband, was gambling all night and returned home in the early hours of the morning, and slept on the couch so as not to wake up his wife. At dawn when he went to the toilet, he saw that the bed wasn't slept in and searched for his wife, only to find that she wasn't in the house.

He heard a woman screaming and followed the sound to the gorge, where he found his wife had given birth by herself. She was bleeding profusely; the baby dehydrated and blueish, the umbilical cord still attached. Mrs Winters had broken her ankle and couldn't move.

Jack Winter took the newborn and ran to the house, calling for an ambulance. By the time he returned, with his baby wrapped in a towel, Mrs Winter was unconscious and barely breathing. The paramedics arrived and administered first aid to mother and baby, before transferring Mrs Winter to the hospital, where she received a blood transfusion.

The next day, when she was stabilised, Constable Roberts and Station Sargent Dwyer took her statement about a woman being pushed off the gorge into the water. We examined the supposed crime scene and found no evidence of tyre marks or that the steel barrier had been impacted. We dispatched a police diver, Constable Roberts, to examine the water within the gorge and found no evidence of a submerged car.

We can only conclude that Mrs Winter suffered a hallucination as the result of her great psychological and physical distress.

'Do you remember Azra's birth?' I asked as I turned toward Dawn.

She shook her head.

'You don't remember anything about that night.'

Shook her head again.

'Can I tell you what I just discovered?'

Dawn hesitated before nodding. I told her about the report, how she saw a woman in her car go over the gorge.

'Do you have any memory of that?'

Dawn shook her head again, completely blank.

The electric shock and completely wiped those memories from existence.

I remembered the story Liam told me about Jack holding the gorge hostage after children vandalised Dawn's tribute. He must have felt such tremendous guilt about his wife and daughter nearly dying while he was gambling.

I continued reading the notes. As the electric shock therapy progressed, Dawn's memories of that night faded more and more. Soon, the psychiatrist concluded that the delusion was formed because of her impeding mortality and that as she returned to the real world; she had no need of the delusion to process the danger she was in that night.

I kept returning to the name of the police diver, Constable Roberts. He had already proven himself either incompetent or culpable in Ben's death, and now here he was again. Was this another example of police incompetence or something more sinister? Either way, there was one easy way of proving or disproving this. I just had to get my own diver to go into the gorge.

I found the notes about Dawn's hospitalisation after Azra was found in the front yard. The doctor concluded that the stress of returning to be a full-time mother had brought about another breakdown. He changed her medication dosage. After another one month hospital stay, Dawn was discharged. This time she and Jack moved in with her in-laws at the

Winter farm and her mother-in-law was designated as Azra's primary carer.

I wanted to ask Dawn about what it must have been like to move in with her in-laws and to not be able to mother her child, but I worried it might be too deep a wound to open. I needed to stay on point.

I flicked through the rest of the files. Over the next fifteen years, Dawn was hospitalised sporadically, each time retreating more and more. On her third stay, she stopped speaking and no treatment or medication would change that. Soon after, there were only annual records of the psychiatrist checking her medication levels and adjusting dosages, with Jack attending every visit to speak on her behalf. It seemed after her near death experience he became a devoted husband and father, the scare hopefully stopping his gambling addiction.

Reading her medical file was like reading about a woman who became invisible and mute in order to survive.

'I think I know what to do,' I told Dawn as I packed up the files. 'We need to get our own diver to go into the lake. We need to prove once and for all whether or not there is a car there.'

Dawn grabbed my hands and smiled, tears seeping from her eyes. She put her hand on her mouth and made a symbol as if she were almost blowing a kiss. I realised it was a symbol for thank you.

'You're welcome,' I said, trying to think about how to find a diver to go into the gorge.

By the time I'd dropped Dawn off at the Winter farm, I'd figured out a plan of sorts.

As soon I got home, I called Alyssa. After we exchanged small talk, I got down to my ask.

'I'm working on a secondary case. This Bosnian woman who came to Riverwood in 1969.' I told her about Dawn and her search for Maureen. 'I want to get a diver to go into the gorge and see if there is a car there.'

'Uh, I think I might help there,' Alyssa said, her voice smug.

'Do you know someone?'

'Yeah, Phil. He's an avid diver. Has all the equipment.'

'Really. Do you think he would do it? The two of you can come and stay for the weekend with me. See Riverwood and do the dive.'

'Okay, I'll check with Phil and confirm with you.'

We spoke for a few more minutes and called off.

Things were coming together.

After I hung up with Alyssa, I took a deep breath and dialled my former phone number.

'Hello,' my brother Emir answered.

I had to fight the urge to hang up. I blamed him for the ultimatum. He was the one who'd demanded Mum force me to break it off or leave. If she didn't, he'd told her he would leave. She'd been caught in a situation impossible.

'It's me,' I said.

'What took you so fucking long?' he ranted. 'It's been two months and you haven't called Mum.'

'I wasn't sure she wanted to hear from me, after all, being disinherited means being exiled.'

'Don't be a drama queen,' Emir shouted. 'We were doing it for your own good, trying to make you see there's no future with your Maltese boyfriend.'

'I'll decide that.'

'Mum wants to speak to you.'

There was a muted exchanged and my mother's tremulous voice on the line. 'Seka.'

'Yeah, Mama, it's me,' I said, feeling choked up.

'Where are you?' she wailed.

'I'm living in a town called Riverwood. Working in the local newspaper.'

'With Ninu?' Mama asked.

'No, he's at his house. I'm renting a house on my own.'

Mama breathed a sighed of relief.

'We're still together,' I told her. 'He comes up every week-end.'

I didn't want her to get too comfortable in thinking that she'd won.

'Tell me about it?' she asked.

I was surprised. I'd expected her to be cold and standoffish, but she was actually eager to talk to me. Maybe she regretted the ultimatum. I told her about the town.

'Maybe you can visit sometime?' she said.

'I'd like that.' I gave her my new phone number and address.

'Emir wants to talk to you before you go?'

She said goodbye and transferred the phone over.

'You gave her a good scare. She didn't know if you were dead or alive.'

'I didn't realise you gave a shit.'

'Of course I give a shit. You're my sister. I just don't want you to ruin your life by marrying a Christian.'

'Whatever! I'm not having this conversation.'

'Fine. Just make sure you call Mama regularly.'

'I will.'

He hung up without saying goodbye. Bossy prick. I hung up too, annoyed. My stomach was rumbling. I returned to the kitchen and found everything cold. I didn't have the patience to reheat it so quickly dug in, wolfing my meal down in five minutes. As my dissented stomach rumbled and groaned, I saw Dawn's diary.

I organised my notes and looked at the time. I had enough time for a quick dinner before going to Art's.

Art lived on a rise near the forest. The driveway was long and curving, landscaped with variously shaped flower beds that were overflowing with colourful flowers. Perched on a rise, a long blue weatherboard house appeared, looking stately and imposing. The Monday's came from money, after all, they'd had the funds to start and keep publishing a newspaper for over a hundred years.

As I stopped in front of the imposing wraparound porch with green awnings, Art came out to greet me.

'Did you find it alright?' he asked.

I nodded. Everything was easy to find in the small town of Riverwood.

'Come in.' He ushered me up the stairs and through the front door. The foyer was all warm wood and antique furniture, with large ceramic vases of fresh flowers. 'Come to the living room.' Art walked through wooden double doors and into a living room that overlooked the lush gardens I had driven past. From this angle, the driveway was hidden behind the flower beds.

'I have tea prepared for us.' As I sat on the sofa opposite, Art poured tea into a cup and saucer. There was a three-tiered cake stand with biscuits and small flans. 'What would you like?' He lifted the small steel tongs from the cake stand. As I pointed, he placed each cake on another saucer and handed it to me.

'How was your day?' He poured himself a cup.

'Good. Good. You have a beautiful home.' I looked around in wonder. The house had a warm, inviting presence with a white shelf on the wall and decorated plates on display stands layered on them. 'Do you live by yourself?'

Art nodded. 'Since my beautiful Amelia passed away two years ago.' He pointed at a silver framed portrait of him on his wedding day, where he'd cut a dapper figure in a black suit. He'd maintained his figure and was still trim, his hair dyed and his beard showing. His hair was slightly thinner. Amelia was a beautiful brunette, her face pale, her lips turned up in a cupid's bow as she stared up at her husband.

'Beautiful couple.'

'Yes, we were.' He smiled faintly. 'We were married for 24 years before she passed.'

'Do you have children nearby?' I realised we hadn't really ever spoken about our personal lives. Art was such an old world gentleman and all our conversations at work had been professional.

'We had a son. He lives in the city. Couldn't wait to brush the country dust off his shoes.' He stirred his cup and took a sip. 'He visits once a month.' Art paused, letting me glance around the room. 'So, how is your investigation coming along?' he asked.

'Good, good.' I'd thought long and hard about what to tell him. I couldn't mention Julie or her secret investigation. While under normal circumstances I would disclose a source to my editor, I needed to keep everything close to my chest.

'Do you think the police are correct and there was only one perpetrator?' I probed, testing his reaction.

Art looked up from his cup. 'No,' he said firmly. 'I read the coronial inquest and those injuries could not have been caused by just one person.'

'Do you think the perpetrators are still in town?'

'Undoubtedly.' Art sighed. 'Small towns hide deep secrets.'

'Do you have any ideas about who they are?' I returned my cup to the coffee table, needing my hands to be empty.

'One or two.'

'Who do you suspect?'

'Who do you?' he countered.

Art and I eyeballed each other, waiting for the other to break. When twenty seconds passed and neither of us spoke, I knew I had to break the impasse. 'I think I'd prefer to keep my speculation to myself until I can back myself in an article. And in order to ensure that the story is published, I'll submit to both the Riverwood Times and the national newspaper.'

'Good.' Art nodded. 'That will provide me with protection. It will ensure that I don't face any recriminations by the powers to be, as they will think I only published not to be scooped.'

'You're not angry?' I asked. This was not the reaction I had expected.

'I think you've spent enough time on this case to know that nothing and no one can be trusted.'

'Can I trust you?' I asked him.

He looked out the window. 'I want to be trusted, but at the end of the day, I've put my self preservation at the top of the list. So maybe I can't be trusted.'

I hadn't expected him to be honest. I had expected Art to manage me, pump me for information and sources, instead he was almost afraid to ask me anything about the case.

'I should probably head off,' I said.

Art smiled sadly and nodded. 'I'll walk you out.' He walked me down the porch and to my car. 'I admire you, Seka. You hold justice as your compass, above all else. Never lose that.' He opened the car door for me and I slid into the driver's seat.

As I drove off, he cut a sad figure by himself on the front porch. On the surface, he seemed to have had a lovely life: a long marriage, safety, security, yet there was sadness within him. Was it the toll of a guilty conscience or just the regret of an older man looking back on his past self?

14-Intruder

I stood from my chair, my neck sore and my back achey. I'd spent the afternoon glued to my seat as I drafted the article. Now, it was finally done.

I emailed it to Alyssa and then printed a copy. As I drove to the newspaper office, a weight was lifted off my back. I hoped that this would be the article that would lead to someone coming forward. There was a witness to Ben's death. There had to be. And with the article being so public and vehement that there were multiple perpetrators, I hoped it would put pressure among the murders. I just needed one break. Something to shake loose and point the way to one of the perpetrators.

I walked into the office. It was deserted. Everyone had gone home. I handed Art the article and waited while he read it. He copyedited and lifted it for me to see. 'Are you happy with this?' he asked.

I nodded.

'Alright. I'll go lay it out on the printing press.' He tucked the red pen behind his ear.

'There's one more thing.' I took out a copy of the advertisement that Dawn had originally run in the Riverwood Times all those years before. 'I want this published too.' If what I suspected was true, and Maureen really was at the bottom of the gorge, I wanted to shake something loose there too.

Art read it and frowned. 'Where is this coming from?' he asked.

'Dawn asked me to find her friend.' I met his eyes, waiting to see if he would confess that he too had attempted to help Dawn back in the day and give me an opening to ask him about her hospital stay.

'If that's what you want. I'll put it on the advertisement page.'

'Thanks,' I nodded.

As I was driving home, I saw Liam's car at Martin Mechanics. I parked next to his car and walked into the mechanics.

There was the imposing man in the office, his name tag read Tanner. 'I'm looking for Liam.'

'He's upstairs with his pop.' He nodded to a door to my left.

I walked up the stairs and reached a landing where there were two flats. When I knocked on Liam's flat, nobody answered. I knocked on his father's door and Colin opened, a tea towel in his hands.

'Seka, lovely to see you. Come in and join us for dinner.'

My stomach rumbled at the inviting smells coming from the kitchen. I felt embarrassed for interrupting their dinner.

'No, I just want to speak to Liam quickly.'

Colin moved out of the doorway and I saw Liam in the kitchen, taking out a roast chicken. Colin waved him over and returned to the kitchen.

'Sorry to interrupt,' I told Liam after he'd closed the flat door. We were speaking on the landing next to the stairs. 'I just wanted to touch base on the drowning case.'

'What drowning?' Liam asked.

'Dawn Winter believes a woman drowned at the gorge. And I've been working to help her find out if it's true. I think it is.'

'You do?' Liam was sceptical.

'I have a police diver who is going to dive in the gorge on Saturday to see if there's anything there.'

'But the police already did that.'

'Mmmm,' I said, non-concomitantly.

'You think they got it wrong?'

'I think the wrong person dived there.'

'You think Roberts is dirty?'

'I think there are questions that should be asked.'

His lips tightened with displeasure. 'Let me know what time the diver will be there.'

I nodded.

As I walked downstairs, Tanner was wiping a part on the table to the left of the stairs. I nodded as I passed.

As I drove home, I felt slightly flat. I thought Liam was someone I could rely on, yet he was still loyal to his boss. As I drove past the newspaper office, I smiled slightly. At least I'd know tomorrow where Art's loyalty lay.

I was home, reading a novel, when I heard a creak from the backroom. As I walked towards it, I noticed that the laundry cupboard in the pantry had opened, and the hinges creaked as it slowly opened. I slammed it shut, and it swung open again. I opened it fully and rummaged around inside, attempting to see what was keeping it from closing properly. A photo fluttered to the ground.

I bent to pick it up. It was a colour photo with white edges, a woman with red hair held a boy of about three-years old who had her colouring. The boy was wearing overalls, holding a blue truck in his hands, behind them Colin Martin. I peered closer and recognised the child as Liam. Did they live in this house? I took the photo with me, placing it on my bedside table. I would have to take it with me to show Liam the next day. He'd probably love to get a photo of his mother.

When I turned over the photo, I noticed that it was labelled 'Molly, Colin and Liam, 1969?"

I was sleeping deeply when the woman from the photo appeared beside my bed. 'Wake up Seka,' she shouted, her voice coming from far away. 'He's coming.'

I woke, my heart pounding. There was no one in my bedroom. I lay my head down when I heard the creak of floorboards. Someone was in the house with me. Was Molly really here with me? No, that was absurd. She lived here in 1969. Dream and reality merged, and it was hard to tell which was which. I heard another creak, the unmistakable sound of footsteps in the hallway, attempting to be covert. What had Molly said? 'He's coming.'

My skin rose with goosepimples, warning of danger. I looked around me. There was nowhere to go in the room. The only way out was through the window. I didn't have enough time to open the window and escape before he came. Urgency filled me. I caught sight of the wooden chair that I hung my clothes on. Standing quickly, I picked it up, hurled it through the window. The clothes on the chair scattered over the shards of glass. I leaped over the window ledge, my foot burning as I stepped on a shard. The bedroom door opened and a large male figure loomed in the doorway, ominous and malevolent, his face hidden in the darkness. He leaped for the window, his arm reaching for me, the smell of menthol, diesel fuel and cigarettes wafting my way.

I leaped away, running. It was Julie's attacker. I remembered her eyes as she spoke of the assault. I did not want this man to catch up with me. As I ran away from the house, I was fleet-footed. Where to go? How could I evade him? I heard him grunting as he scrambled over the window ledge, his plodding footsteps behind me. He was slower, his tread heavy and weighted. As I ran, my foot ached. The glass was digging deeper into my foot, slowing me down with pain. Where do I go?

Molly appeared before me, standing by a large elm tree. She pointed toward the gorge. I ran in the direction she pointed. I could hear him behind me. He was gaining. I took a chance, peered over my shoulder, saw his imposing figure behind me. He would catch up with me.

I reached the cliff above the gorge. There was nowhere to go. I was trapped. I turned back, seeing the man as he reached toward me. He had a bandana around his face, a cap on his head. His bulk was imposing. What do I do?

Molly appeared beside me. 'Jump' she yelled.

I peered behind me. The only way to escape was to jump into the gorge. I turned back, ran off the edge, and jumped as far out as I could. My stomach somersaulted from the freefall. If he jumped after me, I would be done for. I hit the water hard, my feet slashing the hard surface. The water closed over me. I saw him peering over the cliff before the water closed over me. I went down and down.

Molly appeared beside me. I wanted to kick to the surface, but she yanked my foot, pulled me down further and further. She was going to drown me. She wanted me to die like her. I went to the bottom, saw the car before me, a skeleton in the front seat.

Molly reached for my hand and yanked me to the surface, her feet kicking in front of my face. She swam sideways so that we emerged next to the cliff of the gorge, hidden in the dark shadows as the intruder stood at the top, searching for me. Molly placed my hand to cling onto a cliff face and disappeared back into the water, an invisible wraith. I clung to the cliff, my arm aching, body bruised and tender, but too afraid to get out of the water just in case the intruder was waiting for me.

Birds sang their morning tune, and the sun lit up the sky. I glanced around and didn't see anyone. I knew it was safe to leave. The Intruder would have left by now, but was too weak to swim and continued to bob in the water. When I felt too weak, like my arm couldn't hold on anymore, there was a pressure under my feet, almost as if someone was holding me up beneath the water.

I saw a figure cut through the path from the road, and tensed, only to recognise Dawn walking toward the water, flowers in her arms.

'Dawn,' I called, my voice weak. I repeated her name. She lifted her head and looked out across from me. I tried to let go of the wall to swim toward her and sunk beneath the surface. When I bobbed back up, she was in the water, swimming toward me in sure strokes. She reached me and tugged me back to the shore, dragging me out, moving the hair out of my face.

'I saw her,' I told Dawn. 'I saw Maureen.' I gasped as I pointed to the water. 'She's under there.'

Dawn turned to look at the surface of water and gasped, covering her mouth quickly. Tears seeping from her eyes.

I whispered to her what had happened, the attack, and the mirage of Maureen. After I'd rested, Dawn helped me up and almost dragged me back to her house, where her daughter wanted us to call the police.

I shook my head. 'No police.'

Azra still held the phone, looking at me with concern. 'Someone broke into your house. You need to report.'

'No, they can't be trusted.'

Dawn nodded and took the phone from Azra, returning it to the cradle. 'I need to go home. I need to get the diver to find Maureen.'

Dawn nodded and urged Azra to help. They walked me to the car and drove me the 200 metres to my house. Dawn helped me to the bathroom where I had a shower, revelling in the hot water warming my skin.

When I got out Dawn had made me scrambled eggs and toast with a coffee. I gratefully ate, my shakes subsiding. Treading water for so many hours had depleted me.

When I finished, I made my first phone call to Alyssa.

'You and Phil need to dive today.' I told her about the intruder and that I saw a car beneath the surface when I dived. 'We need to get to the car today, before they try to hide the evidence.'

'Who are they?' Alyssa asked.

'I don't know, but I know that they don't want this to surface. That the only way I'm going to be safe is if we prove it.'

Alyssa confirmed that they'd leave straight away. I called Liam after her, told him he needed to come over urgently.

I got the photo from my chest of drawers and the rental ledger, where I'd found the Martin name as renters in 1969, before it was rented to the Winters. Liam parked in front of the house, wearing casual clothes, as he was off duty. I went to the front door and held it for him.

He entered, looking at me with concern. 'Are you okay?' he asked.

I said nothing, instead led him to the living room where Azra and Dawn were sitting. 'An intruder broke in last night.' I told him what had happened.

His green eyes darkened with concern as he listened. 'We need to report this.'

I shook my head. 'Do you remember when you said this house felt familiar?'

Liam looked surprised at the change of subject. He finally nodded.

I handed him the photo. He looked at the colour photograph of his father and mother, her wide smile as she looked at him.

'Oh, I guess we lived here. Dad must have moved us after Mum left.'

I looked at him with pity, knowing this next part was going to be hard. I took the photo from him and gave it to Dawn.

She gasped. 'Maureen,' she said, forcing the words out of her unused throat so that it sounded raspy and guttural.

I turned it over, and she saw the inscription.

'They called your mother Molly?' I asked Liam.

He nodded, looking between me and Dawn with surprise. 'That was her biological name, but she only ever used Molly.'

'That's why you couldn't find her, Dawn. She was using a different name when she came to see you.'

'You knew my mother?' Liam asked, turning to Dawn.

Dawn looked at him with sadness in her eyes, a tear seeping down her cheek.

'Your mother didn't leave you, Liam,' I said gently. 'She's in a car at the bottom of the gorge.'

Liam turned toward me, denial on his face. 'No, she left. My father said she left during the night and he found a letter in the morning.'

I shook my head. 'Alyssa and her boyfriend are coming this morning to dive. There's a car down in the gorge, and a body. It's your mother.'

We walked down to the gorge to wait for Alyssa and Phil. I waited by the side of the road for their car and walked them down. Liam stood slightly away, his back straight, his face fixed in stone. He didn't want to believe it, but I could see that somewhere inside of him the truth was wriggling its way through.

Phil put on his wet suit and the diving tanks. He walked into the water and disappeared, gone for only ten minutes before he returned to the surface. He swam to the shallows and walked out, holding out his underwater camera, showing photos of the car and the skeleton in the front seat, held down by a seatbelt.

Dawn was standing next to her tribute, crying. Azra comforting her mother, while Liam became pale and wobbled, having to sit down. Alyssa called the police, and we settled in to wait. Locals began arriving over the next few hours, and then the police diving team, and then a tow truck. Colin appeared sometime late in the afternoon and approached Liam.

'They're saying it's my mum down there,' Liam told him, sounding like a child who was fighting against the truth. 'It's not true, is it?'

'Of course not,' Colin said. 'She left.' But I could see that he was discombobulated.

I approached, and stood on the other side of Liam, concerned about his reaction when the car came out.

As the sun was setting, the submerged car was slowly tugged to the surface. When Colin saw the yellow Holden Gemini appear, his legs collapsed. As the car wheels touched the shallows and it was wheeled out, he saw the skeleton in the front seat.

'No, Molly, no,' he screamed, as the now visible wisps of red hair glinted in the sunset. Colin stood and ran toward the car, the police holding him back as he screamed.

Liam stood as if he was a frozen statue, his eyes wide with shock as he watched the car come closer and closer. The police opened the doors, and the water sloshed out, with it a blue metal truck that had been in the bottom of the car.

Liam's eyes fluttered and closed as he fell unconscious to the ground. I reached my arms out, catching his head and falling down beneath him, softening his fall.

Colin saw Liam go down and tore out of the police officer's arms and ran back to his son. 'Liam, my boy.' He picked up his head, held him against his chest. 'Oh my boy, my poor boy,' he cried.

Sometime later, Liam was with the paramedics, being checked over, while Colin was being questioned by the police. I approached Liam, checking to see if he was okay. He nodded, looking troubled as he watched his father Colin escorted by police to the car.

When the paramedics gave him the all clear, Liam and I walked to my house where his car was parked and I offered to go with him to the police station, but he shook his head. I could see that he was troubled and knew to leave him to his thoughts.

After he drove off, I checked my mailbox and found the Riverwood Times in my mailbox. I flipped through and found the article I'd written about Ben's death on page three, and the advertisement about Maureen on the last few pages where advertisements were. Why did the intruder attack me last night? I'd expected there to be a reaction when the article was published, but not before. Was Art in on the conspiracy? Did he know more than he had told me?

I was determined to go see him in the morning and question him. Dawn and Azra followed me into the house and waited while I packed an overnight bag. They'd had a conversation with Alyssa and did not want me to be on my own. I was relieved. While I'd unknowingly set myself up as bait, the night's misadventure had shown me just how dangerous this story was. I needed to keep myself safe in order to get justice for Ben and his mother.

15-Soldiers

The bright daylight seeped through the curtains in Dawn's guest bedroom, casting a warm glow on the cozy space. As I emerged from the room, I noticed the soft patterned wallpaper and the fluffy duvet on the bed. In the kitchen, Dawn and Azra were sitting at the table, their faces illuminated by the morning sunlight streaming through the window. Azra's brown hair fell in loose waves around her shoulders while Dawn's grey hair was pulled back in a messy bun.

'Dawn, you're talking!' I exclaimed with surprise.

Dawn's hands were warm and gentle as she took mine, her grip strong and comforting. 'You gave me my voice back,' she said, her voice sounding raspy.

Azra was smiling proudly, tears glistening in her eyes. 'This is the first time my mother has talked to me. I finally feel like I'm getting to know her.'

The emotions in the room were heavy, a thick fog that seemed to cling to every surface and every thought. I could feel the weight of the unspoken questions and the pain of the unknown future, all tangled up in the air around us.

'I'll bring your diary back. Your daughter needs to read it,' I said.

Dawn nodded, reaching out a hand and stroking her daughter's hair lovingly.

They sat me down and served me breakfast. I was so hungry. The aroma of freshly brewed coffee wafted through the house, mixed with the sweetness of pancakes and the earthy scent of bacon. The fragrance of fresh flowers lingered in the air, adding a touch of sweetness to the already comforting smells. We'd eaten sporadically by the gorge, Azra going home and bringing sandwiches for all of us who had waited, but my appetite had been missing and I'd barely eaten anything. Now I was starved.

I glanced at the clock and saw it was 11 am. I'd slept for 16 hours.

'What's going to happen now?' Azra asked.

'Now we follow the investigation. See what's happening about Maureen's death?' I frowned as I sipped my orange juice, realising that this wasn't the investigation that I was pursuing. I was still no closer to finding a break in Ben's murder investigation. 'Meanwhile, I need to get back to work.'

After I ate, Dawn and Azra escorted me home and waited while I showered and dressed. Dawn handed me her car keys when I got out. 'Are you sure you won't need it?'

Dawn shook her head. My car was still at the mechanics and in all the happenings in the past few days, I didn't know when it would be repaired. I drove to the town centre and the police station.

Liam sat in the waiting room, his red eyes staring at the floor. His hands tightly gripped a styrofoam coffee cup, the steam rising from it as he took a sip. He rested his elbows on his knees, his posture slumped with exhaustion.

'How are you holding up?' I asked as I sat beside him.

The scent of stale coffee and antiseptic cleaners filled the waiting room, with the whiff of anxiety and sadness lingering in the air.

He shrugged. 'They've had him in there all night, questioning him.'

I nodded. It was to be expected. Colin was the one who claimed that Maureen had left town in the middle of the night, and now it was clear that had never happened.

The muffled sounds of voices and shuffling feet accompanied the hum of the fluorescent lights, created a dull background noise in the waiting room. 'They think he did it, that he killed my mother.' His eyes were like dark pools, reflecting the turmoil within, and his hand gripped the coffee cup like a lifeline, the only solid thing in a sea of uncertainty. 'But he couldn't have. He felt devastated in the days after she was gone. He called all her relatives, trying to find someone who knew where she'd gone.'

I wanted to still the reporter's instinct within me, but couldn't stop the words from escaping. 'But then when no one heard from her, didn't he wonder?'

Liam frowned. 'It just became normal that she had left. We would still try to find her every year, asking family members, checking phone books for a listing for her name. He never gave up. And then when I became a police officer I tried too, but I just thought she'd changed her name.'

I frowned, finding it all very suspicious. I'd come from a town where those missing were buried in mass graves, never to be found again. Seen the destruction that not knowing took on a person. I couldn't understand how a son would accept a mother would willingly walk away and never try to contact her child again, and had deep reservations about Colin's story that she'd left abruptly in the dead of night. I bit my lip, tasting blood, forcing myself to hold back further questions and instead held his hand, sitting in silence as he brooded.

After a long stretch, I realised he didn't want to talk anymore and wanted to be left to his thoughts. 'I'll check on you later,' I said as I stood.

Liam nodded.

I went out and got in Dawn's car and drove to Art's house. The police were now dealing with Maureen's murder. It was my job to find Ben's murderer. When I drove down Art's driveway I saw him in the front garden shearing the hedge with long clippers, his straw hat had frayed edges and sat low on his head, its light colour a stark contrast to the dark green leaves of the oak tree. The blue shirt with small white buttons was worn and wrinkled, matching the weathered look on the man's face. He waved with a gentle motion, his fingers slightly calloused from years of pruning.

I parked under the oak tree. The sweet scent of freshly cut grass mixed with the earthy aroma of soil filled the air. There was also a hint of wood, likely from the pruning he was doing. He smiled as I approached and put the shearers down.

'How are you feeling after your big night?' he asked. The gentle rustle of leaves and the distant chirping of birds surrounded us. He'd been at the gorge at some point, mingling with the locals, and had heard about my run in with the intruder and leap into the gorge.

'I can't figure it out. The article was published this morning, so I don't know why this guy attacked me.' I reached out and tore a leaf from the edge, rolling it between my fingers. The leaf that I tore was slightly damp with early morning dew, the edges slightly rough against my fingertips.

Art frowned, tipping his hat.

'And I think it was the same guy who attacked Julie,' I added. I'd debated about whether to say anything, but Julie and Art had worked together on the original investigation back in the day. I didn't know what had happened between them, but I knew that I couldn't go back and speak to her after the intruder had attacked me. She was already living in constant fear. I didn't need to add to it by having someone follow me and involve her again.

Art tensed. 'What makes you say that?' he demanded.

'I saw her notes. There was the smell of diesel, which I also smelt.'

Art rubbed his forehead, looking concerned. 'I was so careful this time.'

'What do you mean this time?' I demanded.

'I was careless with my notes when Julie and I were investigating. I didn't believe her that there was a conspiracy at large and had my notes in my work office and I think someone saw them, and connected them to her. Afterwards, she moved away, and I didn't have the heart anymore to dig. I couldn't risk anyone else being hurt.' He twisted his wedding band, and I knew he was alluding to his wife, Amelia. 'But since then—

The sound of the gunshot echoed through the air, followed by the thud of Art's body hitting the ground. I threw myself down beside him, my body recognising what my brain was still trying to process. Someone was shooting at us. Another crack rent the air and it ricochet off the brick wall above me, sending dust and tiny pieces of stone scattering around me. I could hear my own breathing quicken as I crawled towards Art and placed my hand on his chest. He was still breathing. I turned his face toward me. There was a nasty graze on his temple, but no bullet wound. I slapped his cheek gently. 'Art,' I hissed. 'Art.'

He stirred, opening his eyes. 'What—'

'Someone is shooting at us,' I hissed.

The sound of gunshots echoed through the forest, followed by the rustling of leaves and the crunching of twigs beneath approaching footsteps. Art's urgent whispers were barely audible over the chaos. 'We need to move.'

The tension was palpable as we crawled towards Art's house, the threat of violence looming over us like a dark cloud. But I was determined to protect both myself and my colleague, no matter what.

'My house. Gun cupboard.' Art rolled onto his side and crawled toward his open front door, urging me to go first.

As I crawled towards the house, the damp grass squished beneath my hands. My heart was pounding so hard I could feel it reverberating in my fingertips. The rough wooden floorboards of the house scraped against my knees as I entered.

We crawled inside, hiding behind the door. Art entered last, pushing it closed with his foot. 'Over there.' He pointed toward the back of the house. 'The gun cupboard is in the laundry. Key is up there.' He pointed to a hook by the door.

I stood, snatching the key up and running toward the back. My mouth was dry and my throat felt tight, fear and adrenaline leaving a bitter taste in my mouth. There was the laundry with a concrete basin and a cupboard beside it. I found a gold key that matched the colour of the lock and flicked it open. Like most rural farmers, Art had two rifles and a pistol that were used either for hunting or killing pests like rabbits or foxes. Taking out a .22 rifle and a handgun, and grabbing the ammunition boxes for each, I ran back to the front.

Art was now by the large bay window. He'd pushed the couch out of the way and overturned the coffee table, propping it by the window. He reached for the rifle and inserted the bullets in a practiced motion, revealing his history as a Nasho servicemen back in the day. I ducked beside him and inserted the bullets into the pistol. He watched me with approval. I'd had many a hunting sessions with Ninu, ensuring I was practiced with a rifle and pistol.

Art propped the rifle on the edge of the coffee table and pointed it out, watching the tree-line where my car was.

'Will they try another entrance?' I whispered to him, turning toward the back of the room, wary of an ambush.

'Keep watch,' he said, scanning the horizon. I heard him inhale and glanced, seeing a figure coming through the trees. Art pulled the trigger. The glass window shattered before us as the bullet whizzed through and toward the figure, who jerked and fell. The air is cool against my skin as I crouch behind cover. My palms are slick with sweat as I hold my pistol tightly.

There was a thump from the backdoor and Art and I exchanged looks, realising there were two of them. One at the front and one at the back. As if we'd practiced our manoeuvres, we both rushed from our cover, Art to the front door where he ran out in a crouch, shooting again toward the figure who was now standing up. I ran to the back of the house, hiding behind a wall as I heard the back door glass break. I stepped out and shot at the back door, my bullets hitting the wood, and heard a sharp scream. The scent of gunpowder and sweat lingered in the air, mixed with the sharp metallic smell of blood. I waited, and heard nothing else. Slowly, I edged toward the back door and peered through the broken glass. There was no-one there. I opened it and looked down at the blood pooled and then a trail as the culprit ran.

'Seka,' Art called out.

'Here,' I yelled back, holding my pistol in the direction that the intruder had gone.

'The one at the front ran off,' Art said.

I pointed to the blood and the trail. He nodded, and we stepped out, warily following. The wounded attacker was running through the woods, and we followed the trail of broken branches and droplets of blood. When we entered the brush and the soil was soft and with no cover, there were clear boot marks with no change in the indentation. The wound must be somewhere on the torso. We followed further and saw a second set of boot prints. Art placed his boot beside it.

'Size 12,' he whispered.

These were the perpetrators who had been responsible for Ben's murder and were trying to stop our investigation. The dark shadows of the trees surrounding us made it hard to see where the shots were coming from. I saw the leaves on the ground rustle as someone approached, their figure barely visible through the dense foliage. We heard a crunch as wood broke and stilled, hiding behind a tree as we saw figures on the rise above us. A bullet whizzed by and hit a tree trunk beside us.

Art propped his rifle and shot back, clearing his cartridge and continuing to walk toward the attackers as he refilled the rifle. My heart thumped loudly in my chest, drowning out the sound of Art's gunfire and the crunch of leaves as we make our way through the woods. In the distance, I heard the engine of a car revving, sending a shiver down my spine. I ran up the rise of the hill, Art following behind. From the top, we could see the empty road winding ahead, disappearing into the distance. The brush on either side of the road was thick and overgrown, providing the perfect hiding spot for a car. As we made our way down the hill, I noticed the deep tire tracks in the dirt, showing where the car had recently driven off.

'Goddamnit,' Art shouted. Art leaned against a tree, his face drained of colour and blood dripping down his forehead from a wound.

'Are you okay?' I asked. The only sound was our heavy breathing and the rustling of the leaves above us.

He nodded, his eyes closed as he panted. 'Just angry.'

'We need to call the police and get you treated.'

He nodded. We began walking back, but he wilted. As Art leaned against the tree, I could feel his weight against my shoulder and the rough bark of the trunk against my hand as I helped him stand. His skin was clammy from shock and his grip on my shoulder was tight.

'Where did you learn how to shoot like that?' Art asked.

'I was in a war zone,' I told him. 'Neighbours killing neighbours. Afterwards I promised myself I'd never be vulnerable again, so I had my boyfriend teach me to shoot.'

'Even when you survive a war, you're still always in the midst of it,' Art said. 'It never leaves you.'

I realised his Nasho service weighed heavily on him. We reached his house, and I propped the rifle against the wall and helped him sit on the couch. 'Give me your pistol,' Art demanded.

I handed it to him. He wiped my prints off it and then handled it, placing his finger on the trigger. 'You didn't use any of the firearms,' he said.

I looked at him quizzically.

'Firstly, there's the issue of you not having a firearms licence and secondly, it's better that they don't know what you're capable of.' He nodded to the outside, where we'd last seen the attackers.

I realised he was right. We needed to play this smart. I used his home phone and dialled for the police, my hand shaking as I pressed the digits.

The police arrived and then an ambulance. I gave my statement while a paramedic checked Art's injury, changing the story so that Art was the only one shooting.

'And how do you think this relates to the Ben Hayes case?' the police officer asked.

'Because no one was shooting at me before the article was published,' I said tartly. 'And if you look at the case files, it is clear that there was police incompetence, just like there was with the Maureen Monday murder.'

The sergeant glared at me and wrote notes in his notepad. The police told Art he would have to stay elsewhere while forensics collected evidence. I offered for him to stay with me, and he nodded. After he'd packed a bag, we went to my car.

'We need to go to the newspaper first,' Art said.

I nodded and drove into town. It was dark and the newspaper building was locked tight. Art unlocked it and turned on the light, waiting a moment to listen before he entered. He walked into his office and slid open a filing cabinet drawer, taking out a pistol and ammunition.

'We'd better not take any chances,' he said. 'Do you know anyone else with firearms?'

I nodded. 'I'll call my boyfriend.' It was a phone call I was dreading because I hadn't kept him updated on anything that had happened in the past few days.

I used the office phone and told him quickly that the story I was working on was getting dangerous and that someone had shot at me.

'Come here,' Ninu demanded.

'No, I need to stay here and see this through. Can you come down and bring your rifles and ammunition? We need to be prepared.'

He exhaled deeply. 'I'm leaving now.'

I felt his frustration in the loud click as he hung up the phone abruptly.

16-Melee

I drove us to my house, soothed by the purring of my car engine and the crunch of gravel under my tires as I pulled into the driveway. I showed Art through to the guest room, stacking the unpacked boxes out of the way, bringing in new linen.

'I'll finish.' Art shooed me out the door.

I went to my bedroom and prepared clothes for a shower. After crawling around on the ground and in the forest, I felt grubby. I was leaving the bathroom, my hair twisted in a towel, when Art called me urgently to the spare bedroom. I entered and saw he'd moved the bed away from the wall. When I reached the edge, I saw a trapdoor on the other side.

'I think this is how the intruder entered the house,' Art said.

I felt wobbly, realising how vulnerable I'd been. While the doors were locked, I remembered Dawn's experience of Azra appearing outside of the house. 'I think that's how they took Azra as a baby to discredit Dawn.'

Art's face creased in pain as he realised his part in disbelieving his friend. 'We need to secure this.'

I followed him out the door and he went under the house, finding a toolbox and planks of wood.

I was drying my hair while Art was hammering the trapdoor shut. It was only when I heard scratches on the door and opened it to find a German Shepherd smiling at me, I realised we had visitors. 'Lux,' I smiled with delight, bending down to hug him.

'I thought we needed the extra protection,' Ninu said, standing behind Lux, white t-shirt and denim, his biceps bulging as he held a duffle bag.

'Ninu,' I exclaimed, and threw myself into his arms. Ninu's muscular arms wrapped around me in a comforting hug, and I teared up, not realising how vulnerable I'd been feeling after the attack.

Lux went into the spare bedroom, his claws clicking on the floorboards, and I heard Art exclaim.

'Shit.' I followed down the hall. Art was sitting on the floor, Lux lying beside him.

'This is Ninu and Lux,' I introduced them to Art.

Ninu followed me to my bedroom while Art finished securing the trapdoor, Lux keeping him company.

Sliding shut the worn-out bedroom door, I surrendered myself fully to Ninu's awaiting arms. As he hoisted me up and settled onto the creaky bed—cradling me in his lap like some fragile piece of artwork—I found solace breathing in the familiar scent of his cologne, a mix of woody and leathery accents. Truth was, I needed this timeout to bask in his strength after wading through so much chaos and confusion.

'Are you okay?' he asked, his fingers comforting as they brush against my hair to meet my tear-streaked gaze.

'Yeah.' I swiped at the remaining tears involuntarily, making their way down my flushed cheeks, tasting the salty tears on my lips. 'It's just been a lot.' I gave him the broad brushstrokes of the past two days.

His grip on me tightened reflexively while eyes locked onto mine became more focused—fiercer if possible 'I don't like this. I want you to come home with me where I can keep you safe.'

'I know.' I placed a soft kiss on his rugged cheek and stroked it lightly. 'But this is my job.'

'You're a reporter, not a soldier in a war. You're not supposed to be putting your life in danger.' His frustration echoed painfully in his guttural voice.

Musing quietly for a moment, then meeting his troubled eyes I said, 'Maybe I'm both.' Even though the past few days had been terrifying, they had also been exhilarating as I helped solve a decade old mystery and give much needed closure to Liam. I felt like each moment mattered and I was doing something larger than myself.

'This isn't you, Seka.' Ninu put his forehead on mine. 'You've lived this life in Srebrenica. You made it out. It's time for you to move on and live in peace.'

I knew his words were coming from a place of love, but they hit me like a bullet. I would never move on from Srebrenica, not while my father and Ramo were still unaccounted for, their remains in some anonymous grave. Not while the perpetrators who were responsible for their deaths were able to sleep peacefully in the beds. My war was not over. It never would be.

'What if it is me?' I asked him instead.

He looked at me with sadness in his eyes. I didn't know if he could accept me for who I was.

Suddenly the familiar clatter of Lux's claws scrapped along old wooden hallway announcing Art's nearing footsteps.

'Art's finished with the trapdoor. Let's get some grub,' I said, glad to have a reprieve from this conversation.

We all went to the kitchen and as I prepared sandwiches and tea, we updated Ninu with what had happened at his house.

'They're getting desperate,' Art said. 'To make such a blatant attack. They think we're close.'

'Yes, but close to what?' I asked, sipping my tea in the kitchen, the warm, comforting taste of chamomile and honey filled my mouth. The sandwiches were simple, fresh bread and cheese, and yet they had never tasted so good. There was nothing like a near death experience to bring everything into focus.

'We need to go over it all again.' We moved to the living room, taking the food and tea with us.

Ninu watched us from the couch, scratching Lux's head on his knee as we reviewed all our notes, laying out the case fact by fact.

Ninu picked up my notebook and rifled through the pages. 'What about Maureen, I mean Molly? What does she have to do with this?' Ninu asked.

'She doesn't,' I said, taking another bite of my sandwich.

'But they both died on the same day,' Ninu said, pointing to the date I'd circled.

'What?' I asked, then was struck by the truth like a bolt out of the blue.

I saw Art had realised the same thing. Both Ben Hayes and Molly were murdered on the same day. Surely that was a leap too far to be pure coincidence.

'What if they were linked?' Art said. I saw Art's face pale as the realisation struck him. His eyes widened and his hand shook as he pointed to the newspaper article featuring the two victims—Ben Hayes and Molly. The images of their faces stared back at us, frozen in time.

'What if Maureen saw something? Knew something,' I added, my mind spinning as I attempted to slot the pieces together.

'Colin,' we both exclaimed. Colin was the common denominator. He knew something. He had to!!! I remembered the way he'd looked when Molly's submerged car was pulled out of the river. He'd been shocked and betrayed. He wasn't that good an actor. What if he really had nothing to do with her death?

'I'll call Liam,' I said. My fingers trembled as I reached for my phone, the smooth screen cold against my fingertips. I quickly dialled Liam's number, my mind racing with the possibilities and potential danger involved in this investigation. The phone rang and Liam answered, his voice low and hoarse, as if he'd been crying.

'Liam, what's wrong?' I demanded, meeting Art's worried eyes.

'Dad ... he tried to hang himself,' he uttered, his voice barely above a whisper. 'They found him while he was still...' his voice broke out.

'Where are you now?' I asked.

'At the hospital,' he uttered quietly.

'I'm coming.' I hung up and updated Art and Ninu while I shrugged on a coat and my shoes.

Ninu's fingers snapped, a sharp sound that cut through the tense air as he walked towards the door, his dog Lux following obediently.

'You don't have to come,' I said, as Art stepped in beside me.

'I'm not leaving your side while you're in this town,' Ninu said, and headed to the truck.

We took Ninu's truck, not wanting to have Lux decorate Dawn's car with his fur. As Ninu drove, I sat in the middle, Art in the passenger seat. Lux was in the tray, smiling happily as the fresh air brushed his face, his tongue lolling out with delight.

'Don't you think it's suspicious that Colin attempted suicide at the same time we were attacked?' I asked Art, enjoying the feeling of Ninu's muscular arm as he took the turns around the Guru river.

'That's what I was thinking,' Art said. 'They're trying to clean house and kill the investigation.'

'There's three of them at least,' I uttered quietly, as I realised that there were three perpetrators, two that had attacked me and Art and one who was involved with Colin.

'What makes you so sure that Colin didn't off himself because of his wife's murder?' Ninu asked.

'It doesn't feel right,' I shrugged. 'He looked so devastated and shocked when they pulled her car out.'

'I saw Colin and Molly together. I can't see him ever hurting her,' Art added. 'They were a true love match. And he was a husk of a man after she was gone.'

We remained quiet for the rest of the drive. It was a tense and winding journey, each turn on the road bringing us closer to the truth but also to danger.

When we arrived at the small hospital, a nurse in scrubs led us to the waiting room. The waiting room was stark and fluorescent-lit, with uncomfortable plastic chairs lining the walls. Liam sat, his head hanging low, his face contorted with worry. As I hugged Liam, I took in his disheveled appearance—his wrinkled shirt, his greasy hair, the dark circles under his eyes.

'Liam,' I breathed his name as I sat beside him and hugged him tight against me.

He leaned his head against my shoulder, completely limp and lacklustre. The hospital had the distinct scent of antiseptic and sickness. The waiting room was filled with the heavy aroma of anxiety and fear, mingled with the faint scent of coffee from the nearby cafeteria.

'We're waiting to hear if he's going to make it. He might have brain damage,' Liam said, the tension radiating from his body. He leaned against my side, seeking comfort and support.

Across from us, Art sat quietly, his face bearing a pained expression, but didn't speak.

Ninu stood near the door. His dark eyes glistened with concern as he stood with his arms crossed. He'd left Lux in the truck. 'This is my boyfriend Ninu,' I introduced him.

Liam and Ninu nodded at each other. 'I'll go get us coffee,' Ninu said, and left the waiting room.

'What happened?' I asked.

Liam shrugged. 'They found him in his cell, swinging from his belt. He'd written a note saying he was sorry, that he'd killed mum, and he was going.' Liam cried on the last word.

'A belt,' Art frowned. 'I thought he was on suicide watch. They would have taken that off him.'

Liam shrugged.

Art and I exchanged a glance.

'I can't believe he did, that he killed her and then tried to take the coward's way out to leave me without telling me the truth.' Liam fisted his hands, anger in his voice.

'Maybe—' I bit my lip as I tried to stop the words from exiting.

'Maybe?' Liam lifted his head, glancing at me with red-rimmed eyes.

'Maybe he didn't kill your mother,' I whispered, twisting my hands. 'Art and I were reviewing our notes, and we realised that your mother and Ben Hayes were killed on the same day.'

Liam frowned, looking at the floor.

'And we were wondering whether there was a connection.' I breathed out. 'That's why I was calling.'

'There was something strange,' Liam said, his gaze taking on a far away look. 'When we were at the gorge and the car was pulled out, and I saw my toy truck, I remembered something. I remembered being in the car with her. I remember we were pushed off the cliff. And I remember her pushing me out as she sank down.'

I gasped with horror.

'Now I finally understand,' he cried. 'I always dream about drowning.'

'How did you get out of the water?' I asked. The car had been in the deep part of the gorge. It would have been almost impossible for a three year old to swim to the surface and then out of the gorge to safety.

'A man jumped in. He jumped in and got me out,' Liam said.

'Maybe it was Colin?' Art said, playing devil's advocate.

'No,' Liam was adamant as he shook his head. 'This man had a Southern Cross tattoo on his forearm.'

'What if Colin didn't try to kill himself?' I said gently. 'Art and I were shot at the same time that Colin was—' I couldn't find the right word.

A doctor entered the room. 'Mr Martin,' he asked as he approached Liam.

Liam stood, wiping his sweaty palms on his pants. 'Your father is going to make it,' he said.

Liam's knees gave out as he exclaimed in joy. Art and I grabbed an elbow and held him up.

The doctor answered Liam's questions and left.

There was a tapping on the linoleum floor and Shane Otis appeared, immaculately turned out in a suit and tie. 'Liam, my boy. I came as soon as I heard.' Shane approached and hugged Liam. 'How is he?'

Liam smiled with relief. 'He's going to be fine.'

'Isn't that wonderful!' Shane exclaimed, turning toward his brother Tanner, who entered behind him, a five o'clock shadow, wearing mechanic overalls with oil stains. 'Colin is going to make a full recovery.'

Tanner frowned. 'Wonderful,' he said, twisting his lips into an imitation of a smile.

I moved away from Liam, giving him space to greet his friends and, as I did, I passed by Tanner, breathing in menthol, diesel fuel and cigarettes. I lifted my head, meeting Tanner's gaze and gasped, the malevolence glittering in his eyes. As he loomed over me, I flashed back to the attack by an intruder and the way he'd dwarfed me.

I continued walking toward Ninu, wrapping my arms around him and gaining comfort from his proximity. 'Are you okay?' he whispered in my ear.

I shook my head. 'Not now,' I whispered back.

I turned to watch Liam with the Otis brothers. There was a watchfulness to the way they moved, an alertness that reminded her of soldiers in war who were always on guard waiting for an enemy attack.

'I'm going to get a coffee,' Tanner said, as their conversation died down.

I watched him go down the hall, my arm hairs rising in danger. I took Ninu's arm and led him down the hall too. 'Tanner is the intruder,' I whispered under my breath.

Ninu tensed with rage, his biceps twitching as he followed.

'I think he's going to try to do something to Colin,' I said, and followed.

'No, go get help,' Ninu said, pushing me down the hall.

I saw by his face that he was resolute, and ran to the front desk, telling the nurse to call the police because there was an imminent attack on Colin Monday. I opened the hospital door and called Lux, who bounded out of the darkness like an avenging angel. 'Find Ninu,' I said, gesturing down the hall.

Lux ran down the hallway, his claws scrabbling on the linoleum.

'No dogs allowed,' the nurse behind me yelled.

I didn't reply, instead ran after Lux, who was now turning a corner. When I turned it, I heard metal clanging and grunts coming from a hospital room. Ninu was thrown from a door and landed on the floor. Lux barked and growled. A scream. I ran to Ninu, who was already getting up. Peering into the hospital room I saw Colin lying on the bed, his eyes closed, a drip in his arm. Lux had Tanner pinned on the floor, his teeth around his neck as he growled.

A nurse appeared behind me and saw Lux attacking Tanner and screamed.

'He's protecting me,' Ninu shouted. 'That man attacked me.'

The nurse ran out, probably to find a phone and call for help.

Ninu entered the room, limping. His face was bruised, blood dripping down his lip. 'Lux, stop.'

Lux let go of Tanner and backed away to be beside Ninu, his hackles raised as he growled.

Tanner scrabbled back and against the wall, holding his injured arm where Lux had taken a bite.

'I know it's you,' I said. 'I know you broke into my house and that you were the one who attacked Julie.'

Tanner looked at me with hatred.

Sargent Peter Roberts appeared in the doorway, his chest rising up and down as if he'd run down the hall. 'What's going on here?' he demanded. 'That animal is a menace.' He reached into his holster and took out his gun, aiming it for Lux.

'No,' Ninu shouted, grabbing Lux in his arms and turning his back to protect him.

'Tanner tried to kill Colin Monday and Ninu and Lux stopped him.'

The gun didn't waver in Sargent's hand. 'That sounds a bit far-fetched,' he said, aiming his gun right at my chest.

I tasted the metallic tang of fear in my mouth as I realised that there was only one way that Colin could have been silenced—a police officer who used his belt. My ears popped as I realised the danger. Roberts could discharge his pistol, claim that he was killing a rabid animal, and Ninu and I were caught in the crossfire. I saw the moment he realised his advantage. Watched as his grip changed, as he was about to pull the trigger.

'What are you doing?' Liam shouted, heavy footsteps as he ran, pushing Roberts out of the way as he peered into the room. He saw Tanner on the ground, me and Ninu standing.

'Tanner tried to kill your father,' I said, my voice wavering. 'Ninu and Lux stopped him.'

Liam entered the room and turned toward Roberts, who was now pointing his gun at Tanner, pretending that's what he had been doing all along.

'Why?' Liam shouted, as he headed for Tanner and grabbed him.

Roberts returned his gun to his holster, and rushed forward, trying to separate them.

Ninu put Lux down and commanded him to sit. Art and Shane appeared, and then other hospital staff, and suddenly the room was tight and claustrophobic. Ninu quickly grabbed me, pulling me behind him and I felt Lux nudge my thighs, putting my fingers through his silky fur to calm myself.

A few minutes later, we were evicted from the room, Roberts leading Tanner in handcuffs. Other police on the scene moving me and Ninu back to the waiting room. I attempted to speak to Art, but the police officers kept us separated.

As an officer urged everyone out of the room, he accidentally hit Shane on the side. Shane gasped, his face contorting in agony. Blood seeped on his shirt. I clutched Ninu's arm tightly, and he followed my gaze. Shane was the second shooter.

17-Confession

We were giving our statement to a police officer when the doctors came to tell Liam that Colin was awake.

Liam's face lit up, and he followed the doctor down the corridor. He returned a few minutes later, his face troubled.

'My father wants a sergeant in the room and Seka. He says he wants to confess.'

I met his worried gaze.

'Maybe you should get a lawyer before you let him talk to the police?' I said.

Liam nodded. 'I tried. He refuses. He says he has to confess now.'

I kissed Ninu and left him as Liam and I walked down the corridor. When I entered the room, Colin was sitting up. His face was pale, his eyes red-rimmed, bandages around his neck.

'I want to confess to the murder of Ben Hayes,' Colin told the police detective, who had set up a recording device.

Liam gasped, and I clenched my hands, fighting to keep myself contained.

'I want Seka to be here so she can tell my story to Michelle Hayes.' Colin took a sip of water, his hand trembling as he lifted the glass to his lips.

The detective sat on the chair beside the bed. A burly man with a stern expression he flipped open his notebook.

Colin gulped, as if the room was closing in on me, the weight of what he was about to confess pressing down hard.

'We were coming home from a night of drinking at the pub,' he began, barely whispering due to the damage to his vocal chords.

'I'm gonna puke,' I had said from the back seat. My stomach was churning from the excessive beer I had consumed.

'Yep, he's turning green,' Peter had commented, his voice filled with a mix of amusement and annoyance.

Tanner tilted his rearview mirror to catch a glimpse of me. 'If you puke in my car again, I'm going to pound you.' He swerved to the side of the street.

I barely opened the back door before falling out, the sound of my dry heaving filling the car. I was a mess, a pathetic lightweight, as Shane had put it. 'You're puking like a pussy,' he had mocked.

'Leave him be. He's having lady trouble,' Peter had said gently, trying to defend me.

'She's going to leave me,' I muttered to myself, crawling up the ditch. The thought of losing Molly was tearing me apart. 'I love her so much and she's going to leave me.'

'If he pukes again, I'm going to pound him,' Peter had said, grinding out his cigarette.

'Cut it out. He's having a hard time,' Shane had insisted.

'His sheila wouldn't leave if he gave her a good rogering,' Tanner had joked, making a lewd gesture with his hips.

'Great marital advice. And where's your wife? Oh, that's right, you haven't found a woman crazy enough to shack up with you,' Peter retorted.

'I'm a lover of all women. I wouldn't want to deprive them of this goodness,' Tanner had said, making us all laugh. But the humour was lost on me as I lay there, quiet and broken.

'Poor bastard,' Shane had said, and I saw him looking back at me with a hint of pity.

Then we saw a light in the distance. 'Did you see that?' Tanner had asked, squinting at the changing rooms by the footy stadium.

'There's someone in the changing rooms,' Shane had muttered, watching the light bob through the windows.

'I think that's a flashlight,' Peter had said. 'Do you think someone's robbing the place?'

'Who would be stupid enough? There's nothing there. Just some old towels,' Shane had said.

'We should check it out,' Tanner had stated, already moving through the darkness.

'Yeah, you're right,' Shane had agreed, following him. Peter looked at me, then at them. 'He'll be fine,' Tanner had assured him.

I followed them as we approached the building, quietening down and bending low to remain unseen. I was weaving and nearly fell over, Peter helping me walk. As we got closer, we heard moans. Shane turned around and made a crude gesture, and we all snickered, ready to catch someone in the act.

Peering through the lattice slats, we saw Ben Hayes sitting on a bench, his head thrown back in ecstasy, a bloke kneeling before him. Tanner's voice was filled with disgust. 'Sick bastard.'

Ben noticed us, his eyes wide with fear as he turned off the flashlight. Tanner stormed in, a roar of rage escaping his throat. Ben was pulling up his fly when Tanner launched himself at him, throwing him to the ground.

I watched as Peter hesitated. Someone pushed past him, running into the night. 'Catch the bastard,' Tanner had shouted, but we couldn't catch Ben's lover.

Tanner and Ben were rolling on the ground, fists flying. 'Sick fuck,' Shane had said, joining in. They lifted Ben off the ground, holding his arms as Tanner punched him in the stomach.

'I always knew there was something queer about you,' Tanner muttered, his punches relentless.

Ben couldn't stand anymore, collapsing to the ground. Tanner and Shane kicked him. 'Come on,' Tanner had shouted at Peter, who joined in reluctantly.

I watched from the doorway in a drunken stupor, feeling as if I was in a nightmare, struggling to process that this was reality.

I didn't know how long it lasted, but at some point, Shane's foot came down on Ben's head with a sickening crack. Ben stopped moving. 'Stop it,' Peter had pulled Tanner away, Shane Tanner. 'He's not moving.'

He knelt down, feeling for a pulse. 'He's dead.'

'Poofter had it coming,' Tanner muttered, wiping blood from his mouth.

'We killed him,' Peter stood, turning away from the body. 'What are we going to do?'

'Nothing. We go home and do nothing,' Tanner said.

'What about the bloke he was with? He knows who we are,' Peter insisted.

'And he's not going to say anything. He's won't tell anyone that he's a cocksucker. Let's get out of here,' Tanner ordered, grabbing my arm and pulling me away.

'Is he... Is he dead?' I asked, feeling sick all over again.

Tanner manhandled me out of the changing room. Peter lingered, staring at Ben's lifeless body. He had been a decent bloke, someone he admired. Now, he was just a dead man with a secret.

'Let's go,' Tanner said, waiting by the door.

I walked away, the sounds of Ben's pain echoing in his mind. Was it really worth killing for?

As we sat in the car, the silence was thick and suffocating. 'We have to call someone,' I said. 'We have to get him help.'

'He doesn't need anyone. We just have to keep our mouths shut. We went to the pub to have a beer and then we went home. No one is going to know any different,' Tanner said, glaring at me.

'But he's dead,' I muttered.

'I know he's fucking dead,' Tanner snapped, slamming his hand on the steering wheel. 'We never talk about this again. You got that? You shut the fuck up and we say nothing.'

I nodded weakly. Tanner drove us home, dropping me off first. 'Remember, keep your mouth shut,' he warned.

Colin looked at the detective, tears streaming down my face. 'We killed Ben Hayes,' he confessed, his voice breaking. 'And I can't live with it anymore.'

Liam had stilled when Colin described the changing room and hadn't moved or looked at his father.

'I'm sorry,' Colin gasped between sobs. 'I'm sorry for my part in it. Even though I didn't lay a hand on him, I didn't help him either.'

'And you kept this secret,' I said, full of disgust and anger. 'Even though a mother grieved across town.'

Colin nodded, looking shamefaced.

'Did you kill Mum?' Liam asked, his voice breaking.

Colin shook his head jerkily. 'No, I promise you, I thought she'd left. She was already angry at me for drinking too much and not being a family man. I just thought she'd had enough and packed up.'

'And left me,' Liam said, anger colouring his tone. 'You thought it was logical that she would abandon me?'

Colin didn't meet his gaze.

'You wanted to believe that she left,' Liam said, standing up, his hands fisted in rage. 'You wanted to believe it, even though you knew they did something to her to keep her quiet.'

Colin kept crying, low guttural sobs, not able to speak.

Liam headed for the door, slamming it open with a bang as it hit into the wall. He rushed out. I followed, finding him leaning against the wall, his fist against his mouth as he held back his sobs.

I scooped him up, holding him tight against me as he cried.

'It was his fault that she's dead. He killed two people with his cowardice,' he whispered against my neck.

'I know.' I also know that he was crying for more than that. He was crying for the father he thought he knew and yet hadn't existed. He was crying for Ben Hayes, who was gay like him. And he was crying because he knew that at any given moment, he could be like Ben Hayes.

I walked him back to the waiting room, my heart pounding with each step. The fluorescent lights above flickered slightly, casting an eerie glow over the sterile white walls. The scent of antiseptic filled the air, a constant reminder of the pain and suffering that lingered within these halls. As we walked down the corridor, I noticed Shane sitting on an examination table in his singlet, his muscular arms resting on his knees. The room felt chilly, and the starkness of the hospital seemed to amplify the tension.

Liam followed my gaze and paused, his eyes widening with recognition. He tore from my arms, the sound of his hurried footsteps echoing off the linoleum floor, and walked over to Shane. His hands shook as he lifted Shane's arm, exposing the Southern Cross tattoo on his forearm.

'It was you,' Liam said, his voice trembling. 'You were the one who pulled me out of the car and left my mother to die.'

Shane looked at him with a pained gaze, his eyes filled with regret and sorrow. He nodded slowly, the movement almost imperceptible.

Liam gasped, his face draining paf colour as he staggered backward. His knees buckled, and I quickly pushed him into the chair beside the bed. He collapsed into it, his chest heaving as he tried to catch his breath.

'Molly heard us talking,' Shane said, his voice strained, 'and realised what we'd done. Tanner didn't trust her to keep his mouth shut. He thought she was running off to the police to dob us in.' He rubbed a hand over his face, his fingers trembling as he tried to control his emotions. 'We followed her, and I thought Tanner was just going to try to talk sense into her. But when we got to the gorge, he—' Shane's voice broke, and he struggled to find the words. 'I ran out of the car and watched the car sink. Molly started shouting, and you were crying. I couldn't let you die, so I jumped.' He rubbed his leg, wincing at the memory. 'Banged my leg on the back of the door, and it's never been right since.'

'You think that makes up for killing my mother?' Liam demanded, his voice rising in anger.

Shane shook his head, his eyes glistening with unshed tears. 'Of course not. Nothing does that.' He sighed, a heavy, resigned sound that seemed to echo in the small room. 'Tanner fished us both out, and we doused you with whisky, took you back to your house, tucked you into bed. That's when Tanner found the note Molly had left and realised she was leaving Colin and taking you with her. She probably would have kept our secret, but it was too late.'

Shane put on his shirt, his movements slow and deliberate. 'Tanner was always like that, impulsive, violent. But he was my brother. I had to protect him.'

'Even though he's a murderer and a rapist,' I demanded, my voice shaking with fury.

Shane looked at me in shock, his eyes wide and disbelieving. 'He raped no one.'

'He raped Julie Caine when she was investigating Ben's case. Drove her to drop it. And he broke into my house, probably wanting to do the same. And he nearly killed Dawn's baby when he took her out of the house and left her in the heat.'

Shane looked away, his face contorted with shame. His shoulders slumped, and he seemed to shrink into himself, a man weighed down by the burden of his brother's sins.

The room fell silent, the weight of Shane's confession hanging heavy in the air. The steady beeping of the heart monitor in the next room was the only sound, a constant reminder of the fragile lives intertwined by tragedy and betrayal.

The detective appeared, walking hurriedly. 'Sargent Peter Roberts and Tanner Otis are missing.'

I filled the detective in on Shane's confession. As I spoke, he realised that Peter and Tanner were probably on the run, knowing that their crimes were about to come to light.

'Where would your brother choose to hide, Mr Otis?' the detective asked.

Shane shrugged, his gaze fixed on the floor. 'He's probably out in the bush, trying to hide out.'

'Where?' Liam demanded, his voice raw with emotion.

Shane couldn't meet his gaze, finally telling the detective the location of a hunting lodge that he and his brother used, and describing the location.

Liam stood, and I stepped in beside him, my arm around his waist to keep him stable because he still looked so shocked. He stopped and turned back to Shane. 'You're scum. You pretended to be the hero of the town, and instead you're nothing but a thug and a murderer.'

Shane winced slightly, but didn't speak, as the detective read him his rights and placed handcuffs around his wrists.

The cold metal clinked as they secured his hands behind his back. Shane was led away, his eyes fixed on the floor.

Liam and I watched in silence, the enormity of the moment sinking in. The sterile scent of the hospital mingled with the faint echo of footsteps fading down the corridor. I could feel Liam's body trembling beside me.

As Shane disappeared from view, Liam turned to me. 'He's finally going to pay for what he did,' he whispered, his voice barely audible.

I nodded, holding him a little tighter. 'Yes, he will. We'll make sure of it.'

When we entered the waiting room, Ninu and Art approached, faces creased in concern as they saw Liam's pallor.

'I want to get out of here,' Liam pleaded. 'Please, get me out of here.'

I nodded, urging them to help him.

They took Liam, each of them supporting him by placing his arm over their shoulders, and we walked out of the hospital together. Ninu drove me and Liam, while Art took Ben's car. Liam wanted to go to my house, the last home he'd had with his mother, and I insisted Art also stay with us since Tanner and Roberts were in the wind. When we arrived at our house, Ninu and Art placed Liam on the couch. I hurried to the kitchen and made us hot drinks and a sandwich. Liam didn't eat, but sipped at his drink, looking catatonic as I told Art and Ninu about Colin and Shane's confession.

'You poor boy,' Art murmured, tucking the blanket around Liam. 'That's a lot of shocks for tonight.'

We were all worn out, and after I'd made a bed on the couch for Liam, we all retreated for the night, Art to the spare bedroom, Lux on duty on the living room rug, Ninu and I went to my bedroom.

18-Break

I woke up as Ninu slipped out sometime early in the morning, Lux' gentle whining stirring him from bed for an early walk. I attempted to return to sleep, but couldn't and instead sat up in bed, feeling hung over from all the emotion from the day before.

With a groan I reached for my mobile and rang Alyssa. She answered on the second ring, sounding alert as if she'd already been awake. After years of learning to sleep while on the job as a war correspondent she woke in a moment, fully alert.

'What's the news?' she asked, as I heard her adjust herself in bed.

'Arrests have been made in the murder of Ben Hayes and Molly Monday,' I told her. She listened as I updated her on the investigation and the confessions of the night before.

'So you realised they were connected because of the date of death?' Alyssa asked.

'Well, technically Ninu did, but yes.'

'Three decades, a conspiracy and two families ruined. What a tragedy?' Alyssa said.

'I know.' I sighed.

'So much for the quiet country life,' she added wryly.

We both burst into laughter. I'd both railed and been excited at the prospect of a quiet country town when I'd begun my cadetship at Riverwood, and could never in my wildest dreams have imagined what was lurking beneath the surface.

'Since Art cut you loose, there's no conflict of interest. I'm hiring you to write this as an exclusive. I want copy by the end of the day.'

'Yes,' I said, sentences already forming in my head.

'And after you've submitted, I want you back here to finish your cadetship. You're made for investigative reporting and the only place you're going to get that experience is here, at a national newspaper. I want you back on deck by next Monday.'

I breathed in, excitement thrumming in my veins. This had been my dream, a cadetship at the newspaper, but I'd missed the annual recruitment deadline and then when I needed to leave home, fast, Alyssa had pulled strings for this cadetship. Now that I'd helped break such a massive story, Alyssa and her editor were making way for me.

'Yes,' I agreed. 'I'll email you something by close of business. I have one more task to bring this to a full circle.' We spoke for a few minutes, fleshing out angles, and then I hung up.

The smell of eggs and bacon wafted down the corridor and I knew Ninu was in the kitchen, cooking up a big breakfast to get us started for this new day. I dressed and walked out, finding the men at the kitchen table, being served by Ninu, Lux on the floor by the backdoor, his tongue lolling happily.

I kissed Ninu on the cheek as I took the plate he handed me, piled high with bacon strips, scrambled eggs, toast, fried tomatoes and mushroom. I sat across from Liam, relieved to see his colour had returned. He still had dark circles under his eyes, but there was an ease of tension in his frame. It was as if the untethering of the past, and the knowledge that his mother had not abandoned him, and had instead fought for him with her last breath, had given him some much needed respite. Art was to my right, his face clean shaven, his hair slicked back and his shirt crisp. Even though he had not had access to his own bathroom to complete his ablutions, he'd obviously packed well and been able to maintain his rigorous standards.

As we were finishing our breakfast, Lux stirred and barked. Ninu peered through the kitchen window and saw a police car pulling into the driveway. We all walked to the front door and stood on the front porch as a constable approached.

'The sergeant wanted to update you, Constable Martin,' he told Liam. 'This morning we found Peter Roberts in his car, dead from a self inflicted gunshot wound. We found Tanner Otis at the hunting lodge that his brother had told us about. After a brief shoot out, where one officer was wounded, they took him down.

I noticed that he'd omitted Peter's police title, already stripping him of his respectability now that his murderous past was uncovered.

Liam gasped, blinking rapidly.

'Are you okay?' I asked, grasping his arm.

He nodded, quickly. 'It's a lot. It's a lot.'

Liam stared into space while the constable left. Ninu and Art retreated into the house, while Lux leaned against Liam's leg, sensing his inner turmoil and wanting to offer comfort.

'It's over,' Liam said. 'It's all over.'

I nodded. All the men who were guilty of Ben's murder, as well as his mother's, were now either dead or in custody, his father included.

'We need to tell Mrs Hayes,' Liam said. 'She needs to know what happened to her son.'

I nodded.

'I can't go.' He patted Lux, who whined happily. 'I can't be the one to look her in the face and tell her that my father was one of the men who did that to her son.'

'I know,' I nodded.

'Take Art,' Liam said. 'Go tell her this morning.'

I stepped away, turning to for one last look over my shoulder. He was gazing out at the gum trees, a lone tear running down his face.

I entered the house and told Ninu and Art about Liam's wishes. Soon after, Art and I got in the car to drive to Mrs Hayes.

'It's Thursday,' Art said as he drove.

'Yeah, got it,' I said, chucking a left towards the local footy club where Ben's mum was due to lay her tribute. We found Michelle Hayes parked up on her walker in front of the changing rooms, her frail frame even thinner now, shoulders hunched inward. Her once bright brown eyes were cloudy with pain as she looked our way.

'Mrs Hayes, we have news about your son,' my voice softened.

Millie moved closer to her mum, laying a reassuring hand on Michelle's trembling shoulder.

'We have discovered who the perpetrators are. I am sorry to tell you it was people who are known to you, Peter Roberts, Tanner and Shane Otis, and Colin Martin.'

A gasp cut through the silence that followed. Michelle's palm swiftly covered a mouth twisted in confusion. 'But how? And why?'

I told her the story of their night of carousing, the attack on Ben, initiated by Tanner and then the cover up that took place with the former mayor, the Otis' father covering up the murder with the police chief.

By the end Michelle was sobbing, her sorrow a heavy cloud. I teared up, using my hanky to dry my eyes.

'I'm so very sorry for not getting you justice earlier,' Art said, his voice gravelly. 'I tried, but—' he didn't finish the sentence, not wanting to burden the grieving mother with the foul acts that Tanner had committed to cover up the murder.

We remained with Millie and Michelle until they got their grief under control and then helped her walk to the car.

'Thank you,' rasped out a grateful Michelle as she slid into the passenger seat gripping my hand firmly—strength flickering one last time. 'This will be the last time I'll lay this tribute for my boy. Now we can both rest together.' A small smile flitted across her tired face.

As Millie drove away, I realised that Michelle's grim cracking battle with cancer was coming to a close rather soon. Her son's unserved justice had singularly fuelled her fierce flame of survival until she accomplished her last mission. Now it was time for her to rest.

Art and I slowly trudged back toward our car. 'It goes without saying that you have your job back if you want it,' he said.

I looked back at the tribute and paused, realising how far I had journeyed in my persistence to uncover this story. I had successfully solved two murders, gotten justice for a grieving mother and a son, fought for justice and won.

'Thank you,' I said, as I got in and closed my door.

'But you have a better offer,' Art said, laughing wryly.

I glanced at him in surprise.

'Of course, a national newspaper would want to poach you. You've uncovered an enormous story here. You know I worked at The Age too. I wanted to write about things that mattered and change the world. I thought working at The Times would be my chance.' Art tugged on his seatbelt and clicked on. 'You need to leave Riverwood and follow your dreams, not let anyone get in your way. You don't want to wake up nearly thirty years later, realising that you'd let your dreams evaporate in the ether.'

I turned the key in the ignition, my hands tight on the steering wheel as I realised what I had to do.

I took Art home. 'What are you going to do now?' I asked him.

'I'm going to see Julie,' he said. 'She needs to know everything and know that she has no one to fear anymore.'

I realised that Julie had spent decades living in a prison, knowing that her rapist and murderer were watching her, waiting to strike. Hopefully she could finally breathe easy.

'Thank you Seka.' Art offered his hand. 'Thank you for being everything I couldn't.'

I shook his hand and watched him walk to his porch, the weight of the world on his shoulders. Even though justice was served, Art would forever be haunted by what he hadn't done. I didn't want that regret in my life.

When I drove up to the house, Ninu emerged onto the porch smiling widely, Lux beside him. As I climbed the stairs, he picked me up, twirling me slightly, before letting my feet rest on the wooden slats. 'You're safe.'

'I am,' I said, kissing him. 'And now I write.'

He nodded and stepped aside as I ran to the computer. I typed in a frenzy, time disappearing into a black hole. When I emerged hours later, my fingers were cramping, my back was sore, and my eyes burning. I sent the article to Alyssa, a sense of joy and relief filling me. It was done. I waited in front of the screen, knowing that Alyssa had been waiting at hers for my article, and that she would read it the minute she saw the notification. After fifteen minutes of scrolling on different apps, the reply popped up in my inbox with the subject line: *Nailed it*. When I opened it there was an employment contract for the cadetship. I laughed out loud with delight. Even though she'd made the offer this morning, receiving the actual paperwork made it real.

Ninu heard me laughing and peered in from the kitchen, wearing a tea towel on his shoulder and a look of joy on his face. The setting sun filled the living room with a warm glow, creating a cozy atmosphere. He'd been preparing dinner in the kitchen for the past hour and I'd heard the gentle clink of pots and pans, and now the delicious smell of moussaka wafted from the kitchen, the scent of garlic, herbs, and bubbling cheese filling the air.

'Finished.'

'Yes, and I have some news.' I waved him over and he peered over my shoulder at the contract.

'You're returning to Melbourne?' he asked.

I nodded, and he smiled with delight. Ninu's hand is warm and strong as he lifted me up from the chair, his body radiating a sense of safety and stability. 'We're going to be back together. You can move in with me while we arrange the wedding and then—'

He stopped as he felt me tense.

'Sorry, I haven't asked officially.' He put me on my feet, the warmth of his hands lingering on my arms, then retreated to the bedroom, returning with a ring box. He knelt before me, the plush carpet muffling his movements. 'Seka Torlak, will you do me the honour of being my wife?' He opened the box, and the diamond glinted in the light, a tiny star twinkling in its velvet sky.

I froze, a cold sweat breaking out on my skin. My fists clenched in horror, my nails biting into my palms, and my feet scrunched against the carpet, feeling the fibres press into my soles.

Ninu's joyful demeanour dimmed, his eyes losing their sparkle, and he slowly stood, the air between us thick with unspoken words. 'You don't want to marry me?' he said, his voice trembling.

'No, that's not it.. I don't know...' I stuttered. My voice sounded foreign, trembling as I paused, taking a deep breath and walking away, the floorboards creaking under my weight. 'I think you and I want different things,' I finally said, my words hanging heavy in the air.

'What does that mean?' Ninu asked, a hint of desperation in his tone. 'I want to live my life with you. I want to be with you. That's all I want.'

'I know. I know.' I had to slow my breathing, the room spinning slightly. 'You want to live a normal, safe life in the suburbs. You want a wife who will be there for you always, and I can't do that. I've finally realised what I'm good at, what I want to do with my life. I want to be an investigative journalist and uncover the truth. There's nothing I want more in my life than that, not even being with you.'

Ninu watched me with disbelief, his face pale and drawn. 'You can do that with me,' he said. 'I've never stood in the way of your career.'

'I know you haven't.' I took his hand, feeling its familiar warmth one last time. 'You've been nothing but supportive. But I can't live a normal, safe life. I want to go into the darkness and shine a light. I want to find the truth and not let anything hold me back from doing whatever it takes.'

'You don't really love me, do you?' he asked, his voice breaking, as he closed the jewellery box with a soft snap.

I realised I couldn't avoid the truth any longer. That in order to set him free, I had to be brutally honest. 'Not the way you deserve to be loved. I care for you, but I'm not in love with you.'

He closed his eyes, tears seeping out, tracing a path down his cheeks.

'Maybe I'm not capable of that anymore,' I said, my voice thick with emotion. 'I'm sorry, I tried.'

He nodded, turning away. I sat on the couch and listened to him go to the bedroom, pack up his things. He and Lux left without a word. I watched them go, feeling sad that I had hurt such a lovely person, and yet feeling relief too that I had finally solved the ambivalence of my relationship.

I hadn't wanted to admit it to Phuong-Vy, but my relationship with Ninu had been on life support for a few months now, fuelled only by my rebellion against my family and their insistence that I live my life on their terms. Now it was time to figure out who I was and what I really wanted, with no distractions and noise.

19-Farewell

The morning sunshine cracked the heavens as I strolled along the gorge's pathways the next day. I'd spent a fitful night remembering my break up with Ninu, feeling guilty for hurting such a beautiful soul. I promised I wouldn't ever be so careless with someone's heart again.

Creeping closer, an eerie silhouette rested on the gorge edge, intensely confronting the abyss below. The dawn's early rays interwove within Liam's auburn hair. Alerted by my boots' grinding echo against gravel underfoot, he graced me with an acknowledging nod before succumbing back into his solitude.

I joined him at his post, our eyes trailing down into the hypnotic whirlpool beneath us.

'Holding up okay?' I offered tentatively.

'Digesting it all.' His curt response dangled in midair.

I launched a small stone into the relentless river flowing beneath us.

'I find it oddly freakish how Dad was responsible for Ben's death in that vile hate crime but ended up rearing his gay son.'

I nodded. I'd been wondering the same thing. How did Colin compartmentalise his guilt with the love he felt for his son?

'And your conclusions?' I asked.

'What can you chalk it off to? Life's twisted randomness.' He darted an arch glance at me. 'He used to tell me to keep myself...hidden. Made me think I embarrassed him—left him stained with some secret disgrace,' he chuckled mirthlessly, 'And now...now...'

'You're left wondering if maybe he wasn't actually scared? For you. Fearful... of history repeating itself?'

Liam bobbed his head slowly. 'Is it messed up that despite blind evidence of what a lowlife he is, I still want to believe that he loved me?'

'He absolutely loved you, Liam.' My arm twined his elbow reassuringly.

'But not enough,' He choked slightly against his words.

'Or perhaps too much? Always desperate to shake off the ghost of guilt. Can you imagine being constantly worried: Will my past sins haunt my boy?'

'Doesn't matter.' His statement trailed into the chilly morning. 'It doesn't change who he is or what he's done.'

'What's going to happen to him now?' I asked interjected.

'He's heading to prison,' Liam said, staring into the river. 'The sentencing for manslaughter is ten years at least ... perhaps less if he's lucky and gets early parole.'

Internally, I judged. It didn't seem enough for torturing a mother for three decades with obfuscation.

'It just feels wrong.' Primal rage seized Liam, casting shadows over his finely chiseled features: 'Michelle condemned to perpetual grief by his actions while he—' His sentence quivered and shattered-drowned by silent tears. 'It's not fair.'

I stood silently, holding his hand as he cried, knowing that there were no words of comfort. I knew all too well about the pain of injustice, the way it wore down your soul, leaving you a husk.

Liam wiped his cheeks with the sleeve of his top, looking down at the swirling waters. 'You know she was only 22 when she died.'

I clenched Ramo's infinity ring around my finger and half-whispered, 'That would make me one year older than her.' My past swam in front of my eyes — a life uninterrupted by war where I might have been married with a child. Instead, I was unencumbered and unable to envision a future in which those two things would be my choice.

'You know I spent countless summers here?' Liam broke into my thoughts. 'Swimming in this deep gorge, wondering about Mom and her whereabouts...' His voice trailed off as he kicked at the loose gravel beneath us. 'All along, unbeknownst to me, she lay right beneath our feet... This fucking town.' He shook his head in disgust. 'So many secrets. So much corruption.'

'You sound like you hate Riverwood?' I prodded gently.

'I do. I'm finally going to do what my father wanted and get the hell out of here. Transfer to a suburban cop shop. Somewhere where I can be myself and not have to live a half life.' Jaw set and eyes gleaming defiantly. 'I think Mum would have wanted that. That's what she was trying to do. Get me out of there. It feels only fitting that I honour her legacy.'

'Good.' I was happy for him yet overcome by melancholia, I wrapped my fingers around his larger, stronger hand and gave him an assuring squeeze. Shrugging off conflicting emotions,

I tuned in to listen to the familiar song of cockatoos diving merrily into pine trees nearby. 'I think I've developed a soft spot for Riverwood,' I admitted to him. This forlorn town had somehow shaped my purpose.

Liam's ice-blue eyes widened slightly as he turned to face me again.

'I'm going back to the city, taking on a cadetship at the national newspaper.'

'I'm happy for you.' His lips parted into a wide grin upon hearing my news, his eyes twinkling. 'Ninu must be happy, having you back home.'

'Not quite.' A wistful sigh escaped my lips as I confessed. 'I broke up with him. I realised we don't want the same things. He wants a wife, children, and the white picket fence, and I want—'

Almost reading my mind, Liam chimed in jovially, 'Anything but that.' His voice quietened as he added almost longingly, 'What I wouldn't give to have those things. But I'll never have a child.'

I wanted to tell him he didn't know that. There was hope, but I didn't believe in offering fake platitudes. We both knew the difficulty that a gay man would have in attempting to have a family in Australia, in a country where gay marriage was not legalised, and where Tasmania was the last state to decriminalise homosexuality the year before but prejudice still ran rampant unchecked.

While we basked in the silence, Dawn appeared, carrying her flowers and ribbon. She bore a bouquet and a ribbon. Shielding her eyes from the sun, she recognised us on the cliff

—waving to acknowledge our presence. We watched as she tied her floral tribute to an ancient tree that stood guard there.

'I keep wondering about how did Dawn meet my mother?' Liam mused aloud. We know she was dead in 1973 when Dawn moved into our old family home, and I checked Dawn's immigration records. She arrived in Australia the year before. I don't know that their paths would have crossed.'

'Do you believe that there is a world we can see, and a world we don't?' I probed curiously.

A wave of confusion washed over his face as he contemplated my question.

'That's what Muslims believe. I never really believed in religion and when I read the Kuran, it just confirmed my lack of belief in organised religion, but there was always one line that struck me, it said that there is a world we can see, and a world we can't.' I continued, undeterred by his reaction. 'You know, the night Tanner attacked me, someone woke me up. A woman's voice warned me to run. I jumped in the gorge when I was running with Tanner. There was someone there holding me up, keeping me buoyed until the next day.' A sigh escaped my lips as I admired my ring glistening in the sunlight before holding it up for him. 'I believe that those that die come back as ghosts, that they watch out for us and keep us safe. And I believe that your mother did that.'

Silent and pensive, we watched as Liam's lone tear made its descent into the quiet waters below.

19-Haunting

'Come on Liam, bedtime.' Molly picked up her three-year old son, holding him tight against her.

'I'm not tired Mama.' Liam arched backwards, looking at the table where his father Colin was sitting, playing poker with his three other friends.

'Give your Dad a kiss goodnight,' Molly said firmly, walking her son over to her husband. Colin put down his cards, pressing a kiss to his son's forehead.

'Love you bud,' he whispered, his eyes teary for a moment.

'You alright?' Molly asked, placing her hand on Colin's shoulder.

'He's just fine,' Peter said, slapping Colin's shoulder so hard, he bumped into Molly's hip.

'Isn't that right?' Tanner said from across from them, his black eyes glaring at Colin intensely.

Molly had always found Tanner difficult to stomach. There was something about his demeanour that set her teeth on edge. On the surface he was solicitous, gentlemanly even, offering to help her carry things, but his hand always lingered a moment too long, his glances just a touch too piercing.

'That young boy looks all tuckered out,' Shane said gently from her left. 'You need to sleep little one.' He gently brushed Liam's nose, making him smile.

'We'll talk later,' Molly said, squeezing Colin's shoulder.

Colin nodded, picking up his cards, saying nothing to her.

As she walked to Liam's bedroom, she couldn't help but feel something was off about Colin and his friends. Their poker game took place every Saturday night, with each friend taking turns hosting. Usually, when Colin hosted once a month, they were gently ribbing each other as they competitively played, betting 10 cents a go. But tonight, there was an edge, a tension that cut through instead.

As she tucked Liam into bed and sat on the bed next to him, rubbing his back in the darkened room as she waited for him to fall asleep, she pondered when had this strange tension occurred.

Colin had gone out last night, drinking with his mates at the pub after work. He was supposed to be back in time for dinner, but was instead gone all night and came home in the early morning, dropping into bed beside her, making her stir awake for a moment, before returning to sleep. He'd slept in late, was morose and quiet during lunch. She'd assumed it was because he was nursing a hangover, but now she wondered. He'd spent the afternoon in the shed and when the boys turned up for the game, he was less than happy to see them. She'd have to speak to him tonight.

She woke, her neck hurting from sleeping while sitting upright. Liam was curled up next to her. She gently untangled herself, tucking him in, and tiptoed to his bedroom door. As she slowly and quietly closed his bedroom door, she heard raised voices from the living room.

'We need to do something. We can't just leave him like that,' Colin spoke, his voice full of emotion.

'Do what? What do you want us to do?' Tanner demanded, his voice gruff.

'We need to do the right thing. We killed a man.'

Molly gasped, covering her mouth with her hand. They killed someone?

'And what do you think will happen?' Peter asked. 'Your son will grow up without a father. Your wife will move on with someone else.'

'Maybe that's what we deserve.'

There was the sound of a scuffle, bottles clinking, flesh on flesh. Molly stepped forward, peered through the doorway. Tanner was holding Colin by his shirt collar.

'I will not go down because you're too much of a pussy to stand by your actions. That poof got what was coming to him and if you talk, so will you.'

Colin was limp in Tanner's arms.

Shane intervened, pulling them apart. 'You've made your point, Tanner. Step outside. I'll talk to Colin.'

Tanner glared at them both, before rushing through the backdoor, slamming it behind him.

'You go keep an eye on him,' Shane directed Peter. Peter walked out of the house.

Shane helped Colin sit down on the sofa. 'I feel your regret, my friend.' He patted Colin's knee. 'We will both regret last night for the rest of our lives, but right now, there is nothing to do but live with it. You know Tanner. He's a vicious dog who will maul anyone in his way.'

'I don't know if I can do it,' Colin held his head in his hands. 'I don't know how to live with this on my conscience.' He clutched the cross hanging from his necklace.

'Find solace in god. In your family. In your community.' Shane looked at Colin, met his gaze. 'But whatever you do, you don't tell anyone about last night. You know what Tanner is capable of.'

Molly shifted slightly, and Shane's eyes moved to the doorway she was standing in. He saw her, his eyes widening. Molly went to step forward. Shane shook his head warningly, nodding toward the backdoor where Tanner was. Molly nodded, gliding down the hallway and into her bedroom.

She sat on her bed heavily, the weight of what she'd heard pushing her down. Her husband was a murderer, as were his friends? What was she going to do? She could encourage Colin to do the right thing, go to the police station. She remembered Tanner's eyes, now realising what she'd seen in there all along, pure malice. Shane was warning her not to say anything, not to let Colin she knew. How could she live like this in this house, with this secret? Under the weight of it? Under the weight of Tanner's gaze. She looked at the wall where Liam was. It wasn't safe for either of them to stay here. She couldn't save Colin. His soul was already damned, but she could save her son. Make sure that her father's evil deeds did not ruin his life.

She took out her suitcase from under the bed and quickly packed it, then pressed her ear against her bedroom door, making sure no one was in the hallway. The murmur of voices in the living room caught her attention. She silently opened the door and tiptoed to Liam's bedroom, closing the door behind her. In silence, she packed his suitcase and then opened Liam's bedroom window, quietly climbing out and walking in the darkness to the car parked under the elm tree next to the kitchen window. She opened the boot and placed the suitcases into the boot before returning to Liam's bedroom.

She sat on the chair next to his bed, waiting for the boys to leave and Colin to go to their bedroom. He'd assume she fell asleep with Liam and wouldn't disturb her. An hour later, she was fighting the pull of sleep, when she heard the back-door open and close, and the sound of a car. She tiptoed to the door, listening. It was quiet in the room. There were the sounds of Colin's footsteps in the hallway and then the bedroom door closing. He was asleep.

She gently stirred Liam, picking him up in her arms.

'Where are we going, Mama?' he asked, his high-pitched voice unnaturally loud in the silent night.

'We're going to the beach,' Molly wrapped him in a doona and stood him next to the window as she sat on the window ledge.

'Why are we going this way?' Liam asked.

'Shhhh,' Molly placed her finger on his lips. 'It's a surprise.'

Liam nodded, his eyes confused, as he placed his thumb in his mouth.

'Why don't you grab your truck,' Molly said, hoping to distract him.

Liam brightened, collecting his metal truck off the floor before she lifted him out the window. She carried him out to the car and placed him on the backseat. 'You have a little sleep while we drive and when you wake up, we'll be there.'

Liam nodded, hugging his truck to his chest.

Molly slid into the driver's seat and started the car, her heart pounding in her chest. If Colin heard the car and came running out, he could stop her. She didn't know who her husband was or what he was capable of. She just knew she had to run.

The car engine rumbled as it turned on, and she headed down the driveway, peering at the house behind her. The windows were still dark, Colin was nowhere to be seen. She breathed a sigh of relief. He must have passed out drunk.

As she turned onto the main road, her heartbeat settled and her hands relaxed on the wheel. They were going to be alright. She was going to get Liam to safety.

A car appeared behind her, the distance between them closing. She peered into the rearview mirror. Who was that? The car was directly behind her, the headlights lighting up the interior, the glare off the rearview mirror hurting her eyes, making her wince. The car eased off, and she breathed out relief. Then it came forward again, hitting her bumper. They were trying to force her off the road. She glanced back at Liam. He was still asleep. She hit the accelerator, speeding up. The curve leading to the gorge was coming up. She pressed her brake, slowing the car down. The car behind her slowed down and then hit her again, this time with the force of it pushing her straight ahead, off the road and onto the unsealed road that led to the gorge. The car bumped and shook like they were on a treadmill. Molly hit the brakes, skidding to a stop at the edge of the cliff before falling to the gorge. The car was behind her, and it stopped too.

Liam sat up, rubbing his eyes. 'Mama, what's happening?' he asked.

'It's okay. We just have to get out.' Molly reached for the car door, when the car behind sped up. They were going to hit her. Her hands reached for Liam. The car hit into them, a terrific bang as metal rubbed against metal. It was pushing them off the ledge. Molly desperately pressed on the brake, trying to stop the car from moving. 'Liam, jump out!' she screamed. 'Get out of the car.'

Liam stood on the car seat, his small hands trying to open the backdoor. 'I can't Mama.'

They were on the ledge; they were going over. No, not her boy. Not her Liam. Molly desperately turned in her seat, grabbing her son with her arms, protectively curving her body around his as they free-fell into the gorge. The force from the car hitting the water drove the steering wheel into her torso, winding her. The car bobbed on the surface, filling with water.

Molly examined Liam. He was still okay. She wound down the window; the car filling up with water quicker. 'Swim Liam,' she shouted, pushing him out as the water closed over her face. Liam floated in the water beside the car, as gravity pulled the car down to the depths. Molly desperately watched her son through the open window. She saw his little legs desperately kicking, and then a splash as someone fell into the water beside them. A man swam towards Liam, scooping him into his arms, the two of them heading to the surface. As Molly fell into the water, relief filled her. Her son was safe. Please let him be safe. Water invaded her lungs, and she was gone.

The next moment, she floated out of the gorge and found herself above the cliff where three men were gathered around the car.

'We can't have any witnesses,' Tanner shouted, glaring at Liam, who was shivering in Shane's arms.

'He's just a child. He won't remember anything.' Peter held up a bottle of vodka. 'We'll make sure of it.'

She watched as Peter made her son drink from the bottle until Liam was limp and unconscious. She floated above the car as they drove back to her house. Shane carried Liam into his bedroom through the window, placing her unconscious son in his bed and covering him. With one last look, Shane left through the window.

Molly sat on the chair beside Liam, placing her hand on her son's back as she rubbed it, singing a nursery rhyme as he slept.

Seka Torlak Series

Forged on the war-torn streets of Srebrenica, Seka Torlak fights for justice, retribution and truth.

0.5: The Tree That Stood Still

Srebrenica 1992

In a town shattered by prejudice, two girls forge a friendship that defies the ravages of war...

Seka and Zora have been inseparable, growing up as neighbours and best friends in the once peaceful town of Srebrenica. But as Yugoslavia begins to splinter and nationalism sweeps through the region, their town is torn apart by prejudice and violence. Suddenly, Seka and Zora find themselves on opposite sides of a brutal conflict, their friendship strained by the rising tide of hatred.

As the horrors of war descend upon Srebrenica, Seka and Zora's bond is tested like never before. With nationalist propaganda fuelling distrust andf ear, the streets they once played in become battlegrounds. Amidst the chaos, they must navigate a world where friends can become enemies overnight. Will their friendship endure the storm of war and prejudice, or will it be shattered by the forces tearing their town apart?

Book 1: Time Kneels Between Mountains

Srebrenica, 1992

In a town where survival is a daily battle, there are those who seek justice...

Overnight, Seka Torlak's life as a regular teenager is up-ended as Srebrenica, her once peaceful town, falls under siege and she faces starvation, shelling, and sniper attacks. When desperately needed antibiotics and food disappear and are sold on the black market, Seka vows to investigate the corruption and bring the culprits to justice.

As the war ravages Srebrenica, Seka's resilience is tested as she navigates loss, fear, and the harsh realities of war. Yet, amidst the devastation, she finds a glimmer of hope as her relationship with Ramo blossoms from friendship to love. But as she fights for justice and love, will Seka triumph, or will the brutal war tear everything she holds dear apart?

Bonus Short Story: Belma's Liberation
In a village shadowed by abuse, there are those with courage who fight for liberation...
Sign up to my newsletter and read *Belma's Liberation* to find out how Seka saved her friend from her abusive father.

Book 2: Ghosts Among the Gumtrees

Melbourne, 1997

In a city where the guilty roam free, there are those who seek retribution...

After surviving the brutal siege of Srebrenica, Seka Torlak is trying to rebuild her life as a refugee in Melbourne, 1997. But her fragile peace is shattered when she spots a war criminal responsible for her father's death walking freely in the city. Determined to uncover his true identity and bring him to justice, Seka delves into an investigation that reveals a sinister underbelly of suburbia, where genocide deniers hide in plain sight.

Haunted by memories of war and loss, Seka grapples with the raging conflict within her: the pursuit of justice versus the thirst for retribution. As she navigates this perilous path, she must decide what she is willing to sacrifice for the truth. Will Seka find her salvation, or will she lose her soul in the process?

Bonus Short Story: Zora's Story
In the ruins of war, there are those who cling to memories of friendship...

Sign up to my newsletter and read *Zora's Story* to find out her story in escaping the war.

Book 3: Mad Dawn Winter

Riverwood, 1998

In a town submerged with secrets and corruption, there are those who seek the truth...

Seka Torlak, now a journalism cadet, relocates to the tranquil town of Riverwood in 1998, seeking a fresh start. However, her peace is short-lived when she stumbles upon a cold case involving the murder of a former Vietnam Vet. Driven by a grieving mother's plea for justice, Seka begins to uncover a web of secrets that this seemingly idyllic town has buried deep.

In her quest for truth, Seka befriends Dawn Winter, a fellow Bosnian woman haunted by the loss of a friend and ostracized by the townspeople for her tributes to the fallen. As Seka digs deeper, she finds herself entangled in a dangerous game of deceit and loyalty, facing ghosts of the past and present. Will she unravel the truth and deliver justice before it's too late, or will the town's dark secrets consume her?

Bonus Short Story: Art's War
In a time of loss and grief, there are those who pursue the truth...

Sign up to my newsletter and read *Art's Fall* to find out about his investigation first-hand.

Bonus Short Story: The Regrets of Ben Hayes
In a war where fear reigns, love remains unspoken...

Sign up to my newsletter and read *The Regrets of Ben Hayes* to find out about his first love during his service as a National Serviceman.

About the author

Amra Pajalic is an award-winning Australian author, educator, and indie publisher known for crafting compelling stories that blend heart, humour, and heritage. Her work explores themes of identity, belonging, and resilience, often drawing from her Bosnian background.

She won the 2009 Melbourne Prize for Literature's Civic Choice Award for her debut novel *The Good Daughter*, re-released as *Sabiha's Dilemma* (PishukinPress, 2022). The anthology she co-edited, *Growing up Muslim in Australia* (Allen and Unwin, 2014), was shortlisted for the 2015 Children's Book Council of the year awards and her memoir *Things Nobody Knows But Me* (Transit Lounge, 2019) was shortlisted for the 2020 National Biography Award. Her short story collection *The Cuckoo's Song* (Pishukin Press) features previously published and prize-winning stories.

Amra is the author of the Sassy Saints series, a young adult contemporary trilogy set in Melbourne's western suburbs. These stories feature smart-mouthed teens, love triangles, fake friends, and fierce girl power, offering a refreshing take on multicultural Australian life.

She is also the creator of the gripping Seka Torlak crime mystery series. Forged on the war-torn streets of Srebrenica, Seka Torlak fights for justice, retribution and truth.

Amra is committed to accessibility and inclusion in publishing. Through her micropress, PishukinPress, she releases her titles in a wide range of formats—including audiobook, large print, dyslexic font, paperback, ebook, and hardback—to ensure all readers can experience her stories.

When she's not writing, Amra is podcasting on Amra's Armchair Anecdotes, mentoring emerging writers, and delivering workshops across Australia on self-publishing, writing craft, and creative resilience.

Amra Pajalić publishes her dark fiction using pen name A. P. Pajalic. She also publishes romance novels under pen name Mae Archer.

SIGN UP FOR AMRA'S AUTHOR NEWSLETTER

For news, giveaways, bonus material, and sneak peeks, please sign up to her newsletter below.

www.amrapajalic.com

Sign up to my newsletter for bonus content

Help Keep the Seka Torlak Series Alive — Your Review Truly Matters

Dear Reader,

Thank you for reading *Mad Dawn Winter*, the third novel in the Seka Torlak Mystery Series. This book continues Seka's journey into truth-seeking, memory, and moral reckoning—this time through a story shaped by grief, silence, and the long aftershocks of war.

Writing this series has been a deliberate act of bearing witness. Each book is grounded in historical research and lived experience, and written with the belief that stories can confront what official histories often smooth over or ignore.

Here's the honest part: reviews are essential for independent authors. They help books travel beyond existing circles, signal to new readers that a story is worth their time, and keep series like this viable. Algorithms listen to readers far more than they listen to authors.

If *Mad Dawn Winter* affected you—if it unsettled you, stayed with you, or made you think differently about justice, memory, or the cost of silence—I'd be grateful if you shared that response. A short review or rating on the platform where you bought the book makes a real difference.

You don't need to be an expert. You don't need to be glowing. Thoughtful, honest reactions are what matter most.

Thank you for reading with care, and for helping this series reach the readers who are looking for it.

Hvala lijepo / Much thanks,

Amra Pajalić

Also by

Seka Torlak Series

The Tree That Stood Still

Time Kneels Between Mountains

Ghosts Among the Gumtrees

Mad Dawn Winter

Memoir

Things Nobody Knows But Me

Growing up Muslim in Australia

Sassy Saints Series

Sabiha's Dilemma

Alma's Loyalty

Jesse's Triumph

Young Adult

The Cuckoo's Song

The Climb

Romance as Mae Archer

Return to Me

Hollywood Dreams

Vintage Dreams

Dark Fiction/Horror as A.P. Pajalic

Woman on the Edge